THE CAGE

AUDREY SCHULMAN

THE CAGE

1994 · ALGONQUIN BOOKS OF CHAPEL HILL

Published by
ALGONQUIN BOOKS OF CHAPEL HILL
Post Office Box 2225
Chapel Hill, North Carolina 27515-2225
a division of
WORKMAN PUBLISHING COMPANY, INC.
708 Broadway
New York, New York 10003

Library of Congress Cataloging-in-Publication Data
Schulman, Audrey, 1963–

The cage / Audrey Schulman.

p.   cm.

ISBN 1–56512–035–3

1. Photography of animals—Manitoba—Fiction.

2. Women photographers—Manitoba—Fiction.

3. Wilderness survival—Manitoba—Fiction.   4. Polar
bear—Fiction.   I. Title.

PS3569.C5367C34   1994

813'.54—dc20   93–37907

10 9 8 7 6 5 4 3 2 1   CIP
First Printing

I would like to acknowledge the kindness,

community and criticism of my writing

group: Lauren Slater, Elizabeth Graver and

Pagan Kennedy; the patient instruction of my

college writing teacher, Louise Rose; and the

unending faith of my parents, without whom,

for a variety of reasons, none of this would

have been possible.

THE CAGE

CHAPTER 1

Beryl holds an ice cube in her hand as she sits in her closet. The air is humid with the slow heat of August. The water from the ice drips steadily down her arm. Her palm hurts from the cold. She holds the ice, trying to imagine herself in temperatures of thirty and forty below. She tries to see herself sitting outside in a metal cage, a cage too small to move around in to keep warm.

The wind blows. All sound echoes close and loud. Snow shivers across the ground. She sits, her legs crossed. The only warmth for miles around is contained in the heavy arms of the white bears that mill about her cage, curious, strong and hungry. The snow squeaks beneath their feet. Pale mist blows at her from their black mouths. The bears push their wide white faces forward, against the cage. They suck in her smell, snort out. Steam touches her skin. Her face, like their beards, is covered with frost—it's moisture from their breath, from her breath.

She understands that if the cage fails in any way, they will kill her. They'll reach in, rip the biceps from her flailing arms, the bowels from her belly, the tendons from her neck. They'll bite and tear, swallow. Her body will jerk at first beneath their strength, then slowly slacken. Her neck will roll back for their touch as though for a kiss.

Her eyes watch, dark and small, like theirs.

The ice cube makes the bones of her hand ache.

CHAPTER 2

Beryl was the only woman hired for the expedition.

Her father asked about the likelihood of danger on this trip. He liked to know the numbers of things—the par on a hole in golf, the average income of a Saudi Arabian, the number of murders daily in New York City. He confidently repeated these numbers to others, nodding, as though that explained the whole situation.

She found it easy to laugh at his question. "Good lord," she replied. "This expedition's run by *Natural Photography*. They're professionals."

She paused, and even though she saw her father nodding in agreement, she added, "They do this sort of thing all the time."

Her mother said nothing when Beryl told her she was going. She simply nodded and touched her hand to the bottom of her belly as though the organs that had borne Beryl had twitched at the news. Her mother was a quiet woman with small infrequent gestures. Each gesture meant something: danger, money worries, happiness. Her mother understood the world as a place much bigger than she was and accepted without a fight all events that she couldn't change. She lived her life with her hands by her sides, moving them only to express her feeling toward the inevitable when it appeared. Throughout her childhood Beryl had learned to watch for these gestures with the same fear that a person on a dark night feels when she peers at the handle of her door.

Beryl had always been close to her mother, perhaps because she was her only child. Her mother had been forty-one when she got pregnant. Because of her age, the doctors had told her there was some chance the child wouldn't be normal. After the birth she'd never gotten over her desperate gratitude that Beryl had all her limbs, could breathe on her own, had a normal face. She thought it wise not to ask for too much more and took great care with the child's safety. About the time Beryl was learning how to bike and skate, her mother's skin sometimes mysteriously darkened in red blotches, as though large fingers had pinched her hard. Late at night her mother began to sob fierce and angry, the whole house echoing with her cries. Even her walk changed, became more careful, as though she were bearing something immensely valuable between her hips, holding her hands out in front of her and tapping objects in her path to make sure of their distance. Each time Beryl went out to bike around the neighborhood, her mother would sit on the steps in front of the house, turning stark white whenever Beryl took both hands off the handlebars.

Thus Beryl became the first one of her friends called in at night, the one not allowed to go to the skating party, the only one who had to phone home at sleepovers just before she went to bed. Even after she had grown up and moved out, her mother had had her phone in when Beryl took the subway back to her apartment after visiting. Beryl knew if she did somehow manage to kill herself on this trip, then, at the exact moment when her heart stopped shuddering, her mother's uterus would contract one last time.

Her father reacted to the news of the expedition by taking pictures. Pictures and more pictures, posing her, ten to fifteen rolls of film, painful flashes of light from the moment she'd announced the expedition to the moment she stepped on the plane. He worried in this way. He focused very carefully. He wanted the facts. He wanted to hold the facts in his hand like a flat package of Polaroids.

Her father missed the original image of Beryl's mother touching her belly because he had rushed off to get his camera. Instead he took posed photographs: pictures of Beryl in her heavy green parka on the lawn by the morning glories, pictures of her and her collection of cameras in her childhood room, pictures of her in front of the polar bear cage at the zoo.

Her father never did manage to get a picture of Beryl with the bear fully visible in its cage. The temperature that day hovered in the nineties, humid. Dogs panted on leads, a young boy whined for ice cream. While her father parked the car, she went ahead to see the polar bear. The cement cage was molded in the shape of ice and snow; a few logs lay in the corner. The pond was thick with green algae. The bear lay on its side, the color of lime Jell-O. A sign in front of the cage explained that polar bears were not normally green, that their coats have no natural color at all. They appear white because of refraction, the same optical illusion that causes clouds to appear white.

The bear's fur had become infected with algae, the hollow shafts of its hairs filled. The green bear sprawled across the cool cement in the shade, panting, its chest heaving with effort. Beryl knew that its rib cage could encompass at least four torsos the size of her own. She weighed less than half of a typical seal it would've killed and eaten in the wild.

The bear lumbered to its feet and stared directly at her for a moment, thirty feet away, the black skin beneath the fur visible in patches on its elbows and sides. The bear's haunches stood higher than its front legs, giving the animal the appearance of crouching, preparing to leap. Without the blubber it developed in the cold to survive, it looked bony and desperate, but huge even at this distance. On all fours it was taller at the shoulder than Beryl. The bear's eyes blinked small, black, calculating. Beryl moved her hand slowly up and down the outer bars of the cage. She watched it, her head tilted.

The bear looked at her for another moment. Then it turned and tottered over to the swimming pool, slid in on its forelegs with a speed that threw half the water out of the pool. The water dribbled slowly across the cement, wetting Beryl's toes.

The bear sighed.

Her father arrived soon afterward. For the rest of their visit the bear lay in its pool, only the top of its nose and temples showing, still as a waiting alligator, green as AstroTurf. Each time it moved she heard the *slap-slap* of water on cement.

Her father settled for a picture of Beryl and the green forehead in the swimming pool behind her. As her father focused the camera, the bear's breathing echoed down to her, as heavy and methodical as the breath of a person making love.

Beryl looked through all the photographs with her father the night before she left, five stacks of them the height of her coffee mug. Should they be unable to find her body, she imagined that her father would bury a life-size glossy of her instead.

A single photograph showed Beryl posed with her mother. A moment before the camera went off Beryl had looked away from those small white hands, from that flat tired face. She looked into the camera instead. She smiled. Her mother looked at Beryl, her hands once again against her belly.

In spite of all his care, her father wasn't a good photographer. Things got cut off. Perspectives were wrong. Many pictures in the family albums had to be explained: "That's Beryl's foot in the foreground"; "Aunt Addie's in the taxi to the left." Beryl had taken up photography because it had looked like such a difficult art. She had continued it because through the camera's lens, things changed, especially animals. They became bigger, more magical. She liked them better through the eye of her camera. She liked the world better.

The first pictures she managed to sell were of Minsie, her small black pregnant cat. Minsie grew as Beryl stared through the tunnel of the lens at this animal who curled up with her each night. Viewed at her own level, without Beryl's own hand on her back or head to keep her in perspective, Minsie became the size of a jungle creature. Her wide pregnant belly pushing forward from between her ribs and hips wasn't a clumsy line or burden. The stomach, covered in black fur, stretched tight as a drum, became magical, secretive and strong. Minsie bowed her head, her neck curved, glimmering as a smooth rock on a beach. She began to clean her chest with the quiet rhythm of the pink tongue, the milky sharp teeth, the half-closed eyes. The black hair gleamed, matted down with self-possession and power. Beryl had focused and shot quickly, filled with awe.

She would be the still photographer for the expedition.

All the other photographers who had made it to the final round of interviews had been men: tall, strong and confident—the ones who regularly went on these trips. They leaned out of a speeding jeep to capture the astonished face of a fleeing rhino. They focused methodically on a charging gorilla, certain of the power of the darts littering its chest. In the interviews each man had crossed his legs, tossed his arm across the backs of two other seats and jiggled his ankle as he talked. At parties this kind of man knocked over other people's drinks with his wide gestures and stepped backward onto other people's toes. He thought of manners as things involving forks and knives.

The male applicants had looked at the cage with dismay. Each had backed in awkwardly, crumpling his legs to his chest, bending his head down hopefully.

Beryl stood five foot one in her sneakers, and sitting down in the cage, she would almost have room to stretch out her legs safely. Even allowing for the space necessary for camera equipment, her parka and radio, she wouldn't need more than three feet square to sit in the lotus position. That gave her a foot at both the front and back. On the sides she had only five inches.

Though she was a successful professional photographer, she'd gotten the job because of her size. The coordinator of the project had told her so. He was a round busy man with the long tapered fingers of a small monkey. He moved these fingers as he talked, tapping them on the table, pulling on his beard, rolling them in the air to gesture. Beryl found herself watching the unlikely grace of these hands with her photographer's eye. She would set up the lighting to the left, focus in close. She wanted the fingers open against space. She didn't want his weighty clever face in the picture at all.

Professionally, Beryl took pictures only of animals. Animals expanded on the film so much more than humans. Humans didn't look like they might move suddenly. They understood they were having their picture taken. They smoothed back their hair, looked into the camera, smiled.

The coordinator said, "We were a little umm . . . over-ambitious in creating an inconspicuous cage. We forgot the amount of space that clothing and cameras would take up." The whole time he talked to her, he kept his brown alert eyes trained on her face as though consciously thinking about the importance of eye contact. Beryl found herself blinking more than she normally did from trying to look as alert.

"The cage," he said, "looked so roomy in the design drawings." He reached forward to touch her sleeve. "Artist's renderings can be so misleading." He leaned back in his chair, sighed and shrugged with his long spidery fingers spread out against the air. She read the gesture as an acceptance of design flaws and of fate. Later, she would wonder if his movement had instead been an apology to her for this journey.

"You're the only one," he added, "able to fit into the cage with any reasonable safety factor. You'll be the first person ever to take pictures of polar bears in the wild without a telescopic lens, at the bears' own level." His bright eyes watched her response.

He said, "I hope you appreciate this opportunity."

CHAPTER 3

Beryl believed that being small would be a positive attribute in the smaller world of the future. More people could fit in less area, like compact cars. Sometimes, she tried imagining the male photographers in a few more years, as the world ran out of room. They'd have potbellies and touches of gray in their hair. They'd be learning to drink diet soda, to hold their limbs in, lower their voices and eat more grains. They would never fully adjust to their traitorous wide world that had turned itself into a doll's house.

A year ago she had taken a neighbor's child to the science museum for an exhibit on the increasing population of the world. A large numerical display on the wall showed the world's present population. It ticked forward at even intervals with a sharp and definite sound as though the babies were marching in quickly through a door—now you don't exist, now you do. She knew without asking that it had been built by a man, a man who had stepped back afterward and smiled at the way the numbers clicked forward, at the clean, oiled machine, pleased with his clear example of a principle. She knew he had never seen a birth.

The exhibit had also included a short tunnel, like an enclosed metal detector at an airport. The sign in front explained that at the present rate of population growth, by the year 2055, there would be only one square yard of space available for each person. She imagined a woman in this space, a toilet beneath her, a hot plate in front, some books behind. No need for a window—what would she look at? From the outside, the next space over would look like a large coffin. She wouldn't want to see the person inside.

The area in Beryl's cage was a little more than twice this size.

At the time Beryl had been too scared of the future to step through the tunnel, but the neighbor's child had spun around inside it, holding out her arms, laughing and laughing until she fell over and onto the floor outside.

After Beryl had gotten the job, she began to practice sitting for long periods of time in the lotus position. The first few times she sat in the center of her bedroom, but keeping small and still in the middle of a large room made no sense to her, so she removed the clothes hanging in her closet and sat in there instead, the door shut, the light on. It was about the right width and length and she drew the height line on the wall. A pile of old sweaters and T-shirts sat on a shelf above her. A teddy bear peeked down at her from the top, one eye missing. She inhaled the sweet smell of wool, wood and dust. Twice a day she sat in there, looking from wall to wall, holding her legs in. She put the thick gloves on to practice loading the camera, shooting, changing lenses. She kept her arms away from the walls, her head down, her camera pulled close. She reminded herself not to wrap the camera strap around her neck or arms. She imagined the camera's buckle caught, her head jerked forward, her final surprised expression.

In the end she cut the straps off all her equipment.

When Beryl was five years old, a man had followed her mother and her through the park. Her mother didn't tell Beryl what was happening, but held her hand and walked faster and faster, pointing out things of interest just up ahead. Her mother had seemed distracted, but then she was always distracted, worrying about things that could go wrong with anything she needed to do. She was forty-seven then. She wore reading glasses and she put on a pair of her husband's jeans to do stretching exercises each day at eleven with a class on the television. Beryl hadn't realized her mother was frightened until she couldn't walk quickly enough. Her mother scooped her up into her arms walking briskly without saying a word down the deserted path toward home. She could feel how fast her mother was breathing, how sharply her thin hips moved and jarred with each step on the sidewalk. She held on to her mother and looked over her shoulder to see a blond man in jeans walking after them. She had seen him back by the playground that morning.

Beryl watched the man gain on them. Neither he nor her mother ever actually broke into a run. Beryl and her mother reached the steep staircase to the busy street below, the one with narrow steps. Her mother could never run down it holding Beryl. She'd trip or the man would catch them somewhere along its length.

Beryl's mother stopped. She swung Beryl down to the first step and with her daughter behind her turned to face the man. He slowed. She stood, her head set still and straight and her hands held loose and open at her sides. The man stopped four feet from them. They waited. Beryl stared at his T-shirt with a picture of an ice cream cone; a drip hung just on the rim of the cone. Beryl saw the smallness of her mother against the man. Her mother's feet were closer to Beryl's own size than to his. A slow moment passed when Beryl understood all that she could lose.

The man exhaled slow and thoughtful and walked by them down the staircase. As he passed, he ran his fingers over her mother's cheek. She pulled in her head only slightly and Beryl saw from the way she accepted that touch the way she would have accepted all other actions.

They watched him descend the stairs until he turned the corner on the street below.

Beryl lived across the river from Boston and got a lot of her better pictures at zoos and pet stores. She tended to photograph small wild creatures: hawks, parrots, lizards, lynx, monkeys and bats. She would shoot them through the clear plastic of their cages, or she'd crouch just on the other side of the zoo moat. Sometimes she included the bars in the photos for contrast. Her pictures were never cute. They were somehow speculative and awed.

She once tried to photograph whales while swimming with them in the wild. She had thought she could do it. She'd been told over and over of the enormous sense of peace people felt around the whales, their majesty and beauty. She concentrated with more fear on the mechanism of the air tank and her wet suit, how she should breath and when, than on the idea of being near whales.

As she swam forward with the guide, listening to the draw and suck of her own breath, proud of her easy progress through the water, the light changed all around her. The water darkened, stilled and then moved forward so that it carried her slightly forward too, and she looked up to see passing above her—between her and the boat, blocking the shimmering plane of the surface entirely—a gray smooth body bigger than her apartment, larger than her life. Her first thought was that it would fall, crushing her. That the whale didn't fall made her understand she was in a foreign world where all the things she had grown up with didn't exist: arms and legs, hair and gravity, clear light, sharp edges, distinct sound.

The whale glided on above her, twisted slightly in the water to look down at her and the guide. Its enormous face, immobile and heavy as gray rock, spread out so wide that she couldn't take it in as one object. She searched instead for all expression in the plate-sized eye.

Nothing she knew about existed, had ever existed, was important at all. She felt the weight of its shadow on her skin and she began to breathe too quickly, the bubbles rumbling up out of her.

The guide turned to her smiling, then stopped. In the turbulent wake of the whale she swam Beryl up, with a firm grip helping her to ascend in a slow and graceful exit.

"Polar bears are large," prefaced the lecturer, a naturalist from the Canadian government, at the start of his talk on the bears. He discussed their physiology, habitat and what he called their "ideal population stabilization index." He calculated this index using a long formula into which he plugged the number of square miles of remaining tundra, fluctuating seal population and legal bear quotas for the native Inuit population.

Beryl brought a pad and pencil so the lecturer would think she was taking notes. Instead, she drew. As the slides clicked into place on the screen in the darkened room, she drew polar bears. She wanted to get used to the different anatomy and style of movements. She needed to know what was there before she could begin to photograph it. The more she understood about an animal, the better her pictures. She researched each animal: how its hips went into its back, what it ate, what its closest relation was, how it moved through each of its gaits. She studied each animal and nursed an attitude toward it that would result in the kind of pictures she wanted.

At first her drawings of the polar bears looked like shaggy dogs. Only gradually did they become bears. She had the most difficulty getting the flat lowered heads right, the gaze dark and level. The black mouths sliding open, the teeth white and smooth.

She watched the slides closely, the pictures projected on a screen ten feet by eight. She tried to understand that the full-screen pictures showed the bears in their true size. She imagined the illuminated bears moving, stepping down off the screen, posing for a moment by the desk and teacher. The screen was ten yards from her. A bear could cover that distance in three of her heartbeats, its body bunching up then stretching out, front legs reaching. She wouldn't have time to turn and take her first step.

A white bear with two cubs shone on the screen, the picture taken from behind. "This is a female," said the lecturer. "It is possible to distinguish an adult female by the generally smaller size, the longer guard hairs along the front legs and the wider sway to the walk. Frequently, females will have immature cubs trailing after them, as in this case." The cubs, short and round, trotted quickly after the mother. A man to Beryl's left said sarcastically, "Kootchie coo."

The projector clicked and whirred. A bear stood on his hind legs, his heavy face wrinkled back in anger.

"This is an adult male. They are generally substantially larger and more aggressive. Solitary." said the lecturer. "However, I'd like to make clear that there is no absolutely certain way to sex a bear from a distance. It's a matter of an educated guess or a tranquilizer gun." The class laughed.

The bear on the screen didn't seem so large until she saw that the black thing in front of him was a car tire on its side. She knew that large male bears could stand eleven feet tall on their hind legs and weigh almost two thousand pounds. The tallest point in her home was on the staircase leading up to the studio, but at most the ceiling there measured ten feet high. She pictured this big bear in the photo standing on the stairs, its back feet turned sideways on two different treads to allow them enough room, one paw balanced against the wall, its head pushed down by the ceiling.

Beryl had been raised in a city of humans, dogs and cats. As a child she'd sometimes seen horses and cows, but their mass was raised up on thin stilts of hoofed legs. The horses and cows were domesticated animals that wore halters and saddles. They weren't wide and solid, clawed, carnivorous, wild. Since her childhood she'd seen big carnivores, but in some essential way she had never gotten used to them. They always seemed unnatural to her. She could no more understand that much dangerous mass in motion than she could imagine a truck shaking itself into life, its metal skin rippling.

The lecturer touched a button. The screen went dark and then light. A bear swam patiently through a sea ice blue and deep, land nowhere in sight. The lecturer said, "Bears spend a majority of their lives on the sea, swimming in the water or walking across the ice. They are such powerful swimmers they are sometimes classified as marine mammals, like seals or dolphins." His voice was melodic, slightly bored. Beryl wondered how often he had given this speech before.

A click and hum, and a white bear appeared, its chest, paws and face matted down with red blood, a dead seal beneath stripped of its skin. The bear was swiveling its head around to look at the camera with a directness that must have sent the photographer reeling back, then running away to the waiting helicopter. The bear's eyes were dark and shining above the blood. The photographer in this case would have been using a telephoto lens, probably at least three hundred yards from the bear. Some of the more powerful lenses could clearly show a bear's nose hairs from a quarter mile, but this created distortions in depth. *Natural Photography* wanted better than that. Beryl would be photographing the bears from less than three feet, no zoom lens at all. For an hour at a time she would breathe the air warmed by their lungs and live.

The lecturer explained, "This next series of pictures shows a bear's autopsy. The bear was killed trying to break into a house that contained a woman and five children. The bear was starving. The woman shot it three times in the center of the skull while it struggled through her broken front door.

"In northern Canada," the lecturer continued, "most households contain at least one gun." He turned to look over his shoulder at the slide. "The woman said that before the bear stopped breathing, her children were touching its paws and teeth."

The first slide showed the bear before the operation. It lay on its back across three examination tables, large steel instruments all around. Its head was turned away so that it looked almost as if it were taking a nap, belly up, as they were reported to do when the weather was hot.

The next slide showed the carcass with all the skin stripped off. She heard the shocked grunt from the audience. The bear looked just like a man. A tall naked man, his face turned away. A potbelly, elbows, biceps, flat long feet, knees. Genitals. A male. His flensed body pink and woven with white muscles and tendons. His hands strangely warped. His chest a bit too narrow, his legs and arms overly thick. His hips hooked on wrong. She forced herself to look, to catalog each difference. She didn't want to be photographing naked men in white bear suits out there. She wanted to see wild bears when she looked at them. Only bears. The face was very different. That flat beast face. The thick muzzle, the curving wide brow. And sharp animal teeth.

For the rest of the autopsy pictures she'd looked away.

"In the Arctic," said the lecturer, reading from his notes, "the bigger the animal, the more easily it can keep a constant body temperature during the winter. Most of the animals are quite large: polar bears, caribou, seals, whales, wolves, muskox. Polar bears live in some of the coldest areas on earth. Areas even now unused to humans' touch."

Beryl imagined them wandering about in the huge white land that covers the top of the world. The wind whistles and the animals lie down, nestling into the drifts. The snow is warmer than the air by twenty degrees. They sleep within their blankets. Their rumps point into the wind, the snow slowly erasing them from sight.

The lecturer flipped to a new card. He looked up once at the audience and then back down to continue to read. Beryl thought he had probably written out the notes as whole sentences. "It is hard to estimate how many polar bears there are in the world, for they wander by nature. Comparatively little is known about them. They pass easily across the borders of countries and swim out far enough into the oceans to be in international waters. They spend the entire winter on the ice, searching for seals, wandering across time and date zones. It is unusual for a single country to locate a bear again once it has been tagged."

Beryl had seen pictures of a bear swimming twenty miles from shore, stroking onward. The barrel of its head showed, the dark wet nose, twisting ears; behind it, the slow V of its wake rolling out across the water was the only clue to its passage.

"A polar bear can catch a seal in the water by rising suddenly from beneath," said the lecturer, shifting his weight to his left foot. "On land it can toss a four-hundred-pound seal up into the air. It can run as fast as a horse and knock the back of a beluga whale's head off with a single swipe of its paw."

Beryl held out her arm, flexed it. She could, she figured, toss a twenty-pound chair into the air with one arm, maybe even a thirty-pound chair in an emergency. She didn't know, she'd never tried. Large actions embarrassed her. Unlike the men who'd been her competitors, she had never tested the limits of her strength. She had concentrated on exactly how much could be given away or lost, and what was the very minimum.

CHAPTER 4

Beryl had been born with a loneliness she didn't understand until she was well into college. By age five she'd learned to sit quietly, watching the six o'clock news all the way through with her father. She'd seen scenes of national destruction and confusion flash across the screen, the narrator's voice serious and deep. She'd learned to go on long walks with her mother, keeping her arms slack and close to her body like her mother, moving them only to grasp things or hold people back from herself in crowds, to make small gestures of acceptance or refusal. She'd been told so frequently of how little her parents could afford, she'd learned to think of herself as an unwise luxury.

During freshman year at college, Beryl met Elsie, an emaciated, graceful woman. Beryl admired Elsie's tired floating walk, her pared-down body, the way she pulled in her skirts to cut past the lunch line. Elsie sometimes brought back cookies or brownies for Beryl and smiled gently while her friend ate them. Elsie seldom ate, and when she did, she nibbled on the edges of things in a way that suggested she was only eating to be polite. Beryl thought Elsie stronger than anyone she'd ever met, without needs or desires, capable of surviving anywhere.

Beryl began to eat less. She'd come to see all the waste in what she ate and soon, when looking down at her body, she saw all the pale, hanging flesh. Needing less satisfied her. No one could take from her what she didn't want. She ate only when Elsie did. They went everywhere together, strengthening each other. No man ever came between them, for no man could have fit into the harshness of their regime or the height of their ambition.

Beryl began to understand her own body as the enemy, her hunger as an illusion. She planned out her daily meal each morning, imagining how each morsel would smell in the bowl, feel against her teeth, down her throat, and yet longing even more to be like Elsie and not desire it at all. She kept her hands in her pockets during class so she could touch her belly and thighs, analyzing, appraising. When her hips became those of a young boy's she felt happy; when her face changed to something elegant and elemental she felt euphoric. She didn't care that her breath smelled of decay, that her vision swam when she stood up too quickly, that she needed long afternoon naps during which she could roll up out of herself and look down at the wrinkle her body made, almost completely erased.

During this time, her vision of ideal femininity was naked of extra weight, of clothes, and of need. It stood lithe and strong as a cat, wild and free of anything offered by others.

Elsie came down with pneumonia sophomore year and had to drop out. The doctors told her parents to make her gain twenty pounds before they let her go back to school. She never came back. Slowly, Beryl found herself eating some, eating more—still not enough, but she no longer lost weight. For years after that she thought she had a hunger, a laziness, much bigger than most people's. Only slowly had she taught herself to eat normally, to believe she had the right.

For her first apartment away from home, made possible once she'd experienced some success with her photography, she'd been determined to live opulently and find the largest space possible for the money. But once she'd confronted the enormous swelling areas she'd have to learn to expand into, to fill with her taste and her emotions and herself, she'd decided to choose a smaller place close to the subway.

Beryl had always envied men, the ease of their bodies running forward, strong as animals, uncontested hunger palpable as a rock in their mouths. She'd always wanted to be strong and fast and to lean back in her chair feeling dangerously muscular, to know the world was set up for her. Men had an easier time at jobs, at home, at parties. They joked and all the women laughed obediently, startled at the beauty of the men's faces shifting with unquestioned ease.

Beryl imagined herself flipping a four-hundred-pound seal

up into the air with one hand. She had a neighbor almost that big. He must weigh at least three-fifty and was very hairy. He could never shave all the rolls on his neck; hair stuck out of the creases like the legs of bugs. She imagined herself stalking her neighbor, the breath in her chest coming as a distinct wind, her shoulders wide as a door. She lowered her head and felt the fur grow thick and warm across her back, her head become wider and flatter. She charged, her body swinging forward with an ease she'd never known. The seal, her neighbor, a single curve of muscled fat, roared up, tried to turn, to escape to the hole in the ice beside him. She shoved her paw, wide as a dinner plate, under him, flexed her arm. Her neighbor flipped once neatly through the air, forming an almost complete ring with his body. He fell stunned. She stalked leisurely forward, salivating, raising her arm again. She felt the power of her size.

Beryl had grown into a short thin woman who moved about the subjects of her photography with an easy silence that alarmed none of them, not even the wild injured animals the zoo sometimes cared for. These creatures, eyes dark with pain, faces bleeding from charging the unfamiliar metal bars, stood trembling in the darkest corners. She'd seen animals like these kill themselves with fear, deer leaping upward to slam their heads against the bars again and again, trying to get away from this strange place. Beryl made no sudden movements to start that terror, but neither did she stand rigidly still like a hunter. She relaxed and moved slowly, focused her cameras without threat. She breathed as they breathed, stood heavy and patient as though she were also captive. She didn't use pet names or baby sounds, didn't hold out empty hands. The animals watched her calming movements, heard soft clicks, patient whirrs, the exhale of her sneakers. The animals' thin-wired ribs shook slightly with each breath.

CHAPTER 5

Her parents never fought outright. They never called each other names, raised their voices, or made wide angry gestures. They fought silently, with stony faces and hardened voices that called each other "honey." Their silences lasted entire evenings broken only as they cleared their throats over the voices on the television.

Beryl remembered one dinner when into the long silence her mother said, "Well, I had a fine day. Thank you for asking."

Her father laughed, a harsh sound, more like a bark.

Beryl watched the floor, trying to make faces out of the yellow flecks in the linoleum. The silence unrolled again, the tension greater and greater. Beryl couldn't see any faces in the linoleum. Beneath the table she saw only her parents' feet heavy and set on the floor. Beryl didn't look up.

Years later Beryl asked her mother why they hadn't fought outright and her mother said, "We assumed fights would be bad for a child to see." Beryl asked if they'd ever fought in private and her mother answered proudly, "Oh no, we always tried to be civilized about it."

As a child she'd dreamt of her parents ripping each other's bellies out, popping eyeballs, tearing livers and lungs. Surprisingly, the emotion she'd felt when she awoke had been relief.

Absolute zero is minus two hundred and seventy-three degrees Celsius. Nothing can get colder or more still. Atoms slow, then stop. That is absolute death, not even the chance for life, for change or energy at the lowest level. Scientists compete to achieve that coldness in their metals, in their labs, with large machines, powerful computers. Beryl read about it in the newspaper, while she sat in the park along the river. Yet no scientist has theorized an absolute highest temperature, the upper limit for material to exist without exploding into sheer energy. The center of the sun is somewhere around fifteen million degrees. With more pressure to hold things together it could get even hotter than that.

Life on this planet thrives so much closer to the least amount of heat, of movement and energy. Closer to the absolute black stillness of space and death, far from the white of the sun. Polar bears are some of the creatures best adapted to this cold. At minus twenty degrees Celsius they lie down with their rears to the wind; at minus forty they cover their faces. At that temperature metal becomes brittle, vodka freezes, a rose shatters.

White fur, black mouths. The bears thrive in the cold, padding slowly across the Arctic.

Beryl knew that in the future world of small things, the polar bear would probably not exist. The greenhouse effect will warm the North Pole by up to nine degrees. The ice that the bears live on during the winter won't form until later in the year and will melt earlier, depositing the bears one by one into a bay a thousand miles wide. The seals that the bears live on won't be able to survive without the firm ice. They will have nowhere to sleep at night, nowhere to birth their calves. They'll swim, exhausted in the slowly freezing water, pregnant, wiggling their weight onto stiffening ice not quite ready to take them. The ice will bend slowly beneath them until the seals are once again left swimming. They'll drown, the weight of their unborn calves spiraling them down in the dark arctic waters.

The cod that the seals eat live off the algae that grows on the ice. The algae will have no place to grow. The Arctic is a rigid world: only a few species live there year-round, can thrive in its short growing season. In the Arctic the tire slashes of a single truck stay for years; the winter ice only deepens them. The ever-increasing marks of humanity—the tracks of snowmobiles, bulldozers, pipelines—are easily seen. In a climate where the camps from the early polar explorers have frozen into permanent museums, where their huskies still lie curled, their hair fluttering in the wind, where a human shit takes thirty years to disappear, where the smell from a seal's corpse can last for a hundred frenzied arctic summers—in a climate like that a single tossed Coke can could outlive civilization.

The ice that melts from both poles as a result of the greenhouse effect will fill the oceans, raise the waters. Beryl lived in Boston, a harbor town. When she walked along the streets, she imagined the tops of the trees swaying gently with the water, cushions floating by, a child's toy slapping against the roof of a steeple. The light flickered, blue and solid.

The water encroaches on all coasts. Weather patterns change. The Great Plains become desert. Food prices rocket up. Winter becomes more hesitant, with plants trying to grow in February. Annual migrations are confused and freak storms appear: thunder in January, blizzards in May. Some species—polar bears, moose, salmon—are wiped out. Others—cockroaches, rats, sea gulls—propagate wildly.

This was the unbalanced, wounded world Beryl expected in the future; this was the world she thought she'd been made for. A world meant only for small, patient survivors, all things wondrous left only in books, the photographs strange as fables.

That's why she wanted to photograph the polar bear. She didn't want to leave behind a picture of herself, or a gravestone, or a résumé. She didn't want to pass on her genes or write a book or climb a large mountain. She simply wanted to have taken photographs of a creature awful and strange. A creature who even when caged would be outside of all human containers.

From where Beryl sat in her lotus position, practicing, she imagined she saw the long face of the bear through the bars of the cage. Its cage, her cage. She focused her camera on the creature. It lumbered slowly toward the warm smell of her life. She clicked the camera at every step along the way.

CHAPTER 6

Beryl used to be scared of many things. Chemicals, cars, nuclear war, religion, rusty nails, the ozone layer, AIDS. She would quicken her pace when crossing the street, for she could hear the car accelerating round the corner that would leave her limp and loose as though she were finally relaxing. At the dentist's she would concentrate on her teeth and gums so much that when the first touch of the metal pick came it would puncture her consciousness like the cough of an explosion. During the day she would sometimes lie down in privacy, sobbing in anger for all the fear that filled her soul.

She'd had an ulcer at the age of sixteen. Looking at a poster of one in her doctor's office, she'd felt satisfied that her body was dissolving under the pressure as she thought it must, as she thought the world must also dissolve.

Throughout her life she'd done all she could to hide her fear, to pretend it wasn't so strong. Gradually she became the owner of a blank face, controlled hands, a careful voice. She took a chemistry class, drove cars, ate unwashed fruit. She led a normal life, forcing her limbs loose and the smile on her face open and constant like some strange fighting fish. But at night she clutched her belly like her mother, for the uncertainties that were her fate.

During the day she took pictures, like her father, so she could hold her motionless colored world in her hands and no one could take it away, so no one could change the glimpses of larger moments she had caught, not even if she died tomorrow.

At one point she'd taken over a hundred pictures of her room to create a large collage that she glued to her ceiling. Each picture, with all the restrained simplicity of a still life, hinted at things much larger. Looking up at that collage at night Beryl felt peace, for she knew that part of herself was revealed as magical, unfrightened, brave.

Beryl was no longer terrified of death. Not since last year when she skidded a full and lazy circle across four lanes of traffic two days before Christmas.

She'd been scared before the skid. Two inches of slush covered the interstate and more snow was falling. She hunched over the wheel, neck tense, head forward. The skid happened at the end of her first hour out of Boston. She was in the left lane and saw a glimmer of black beneath the tires of the car ahead of her.

Ice, she thought, black ice, and then her car swayed. She felt an intense warmth fill her body and she thought briefly of unrolling the window. She turned into the skid as she'd always been told to do and the car began its slow pirouette across four lanes. She saw the flat scared faces of people looking her way from nearby cars. Her own face, she thought, must be flushed. The car spun farther and she floated backward on the interstate watching the headlights of approaching cars through the slowly falling snow. One set of headlights shone much larger than the others and she heard herself say, "Truck." Staring into the headlights she saw the familiar image of herself dying: her body much older, her face turned away. She saw this image of her death change to herself at twenty-nine. Her body as it sat now, her hands loose on this wheel, the clothes she wore, the expression she showed. She had a feeling within her body almost of peace. The sensation of warmth was gone.

Her car slowed, stopping in the right-hand lane. It faced directly backward, toward the oncoming truck. Her hand moved to the stick shift, threw the car into reverse. It rolled back into the breakdown lane and stopped. The car trembled slightly as the truck roared by.

She rolled the window down, noticed with surprise she wasn't shaking. The wet smell of pine blew into the car and she admired the snow-covered trees by the side of the road. Their silent beauty startled her. Her vision seemed much clearer. Then she opened the door and vomited onto the snow all that remained of her lunch. Nothing solid came up. The taste at the back of her throat seemed so harsh, like hawking blood. She couldn't remember the last time she'd been sick.

Looking down at that liquid melting through the snow she understood for the first time that this was exactly how it would happen. A normal day, a normal activity and then— death. This idea was new to her. She mulled it over, the wet flakes falling onto her hair, her hand on the door handle, listening to the heavy sounds of the cars plowing by. She thought she must have survived other, less obvious brushes with death—her foot stepping over the soap in the shower, a fever breaking, a bulging can of beans thrown away. They must be happening all the time and she hadn't noticed. Before, death had always seemed so very unnatural, so extreme and unfair, foreign to her life.

She rubbed some clean snow on her forehead and then swished some around in her mouth. Once the beauty of the trees had begun to seem less severe, she closed the door, cautiously turned the car around and looked over her shoulder into traffic as she waited to merge back in.

For several days after that she slept longer than normal, and the simplest food tasted wonderful. It was a long time before she realized that her harshest fears had slid behind her somewhere in that pirouette and had been left lying across the snow behind her like a body.

Two weeks after the skid, Beryl decided to try to photograph a fox that she'd heard lived on one of the large estates in Brookline. She crept up the quarter-mile driveway in the predawn to lie tucked in tight against a log near the fox's den. The many lit signs saying PRIVATE PROPERTY, SURVEILLANCE

DEVICES scared her far more than the fox. For the first half hour she pictured men in black uniforms running through the woods toward her cradling guns, but then she countered it with the image of a small clot of blood heading toward her brain or heart, her motionless shock, her slackening face, the camera sliding out of her hands. That, she realized, was a much more likely threat.

Lying on her back, she watched the light change slowly in the sky behind the bare winter treetops. A small creature, perhaps a mouse, rustled slowly through the leaves to her left, but she couldn't see what it was, for she kept the camera pasted to her eye. Her legs went to sleep, and then her back and neck, and still she held the camera to her face, her finger on the button, pointing up to where the fox would most likely appear. She passed into a quiet musing state where she noticed many things without thinking about them. She heard many creatures without feeling panic, forgot her fear of the men.

She heard nothing different beforehand. She saw only some red fur glistening with dew, large brown startled eyes looking down at her and a small black nose. The camera clicked and the fox leaped over her, one light hard paw pushing off her hand. The picture showed wild beauty, the color of the fur incandescent against the dark leaves, the intelligent eyes, the quiet dawn.

Death, Beryl realized, wasn't waiting for her especially, but it would get her no matter what she did.

A month later, on a bulletin board at the office, she saw a

flyer about the polar bear expedition in the fall. Her magazine contract would end in time. She thought if she didn't do it right away, she never would. She applied for the job.

Beryl knew why she'd been chosen, why size was an issue, why the cage hadn't just been made as big as possible, big enough for a whole group of male photographers running from one side to the other, holding their cameras out in front, excited by the nearness of their quarry, the number of their prey, yelling scores to one another, a radio playing in the center of the cage.

Natural Photography didn't want her there. The bears didn't want her there. Most importantly, the pictures could not show her there at all.

A photograph of nature must always appear as if there were no humans, not even a photographer, within a hundred miles. The viewer must feel that the picture captured the animal and its world without people, urban sprawl and toxic runoff. Here, the world glimmered, pristine and natural, wild and dangerous.

The point was to take up as little room as possible so the bears would act normally, ignoring her. She was there simply to recognize the truth, point the lens, push the button. To be silent, still and small. She felt sure the magazine would have preferred to rig up a radio-controlled camera rather than have her interfering with the polar bears, in the cage, at risk. But *Natural Photography* was famous for its photographs. The pictures could not be less than perfect. Instead of the radio-controlled camera, the magazine had settled for the most compact, quiet photographer it could find.

Two nights before she left, a friend, Sara, had invited Beryl to a party during which she toasted Beryl for her "bravery." During the toast Sara had called Beryl "the bear woman." If it had been just one or two strangers there, Beryl wouldn't have minded the label, but there were at least twenty people in Sara's living room, not many she knew, and both the women and men stared at Beryl as though she were an artifact the expedition had brought back. The air in the room seemed very close, very warm. Beryl longed to get outside, to cool down. After Sara had made the toast there had been a pause and the people had continued to look at her.

Beryl was obviously supposed to do something. In this kind of situation her father would always tell a joke, something old and hackneyed that half the audience already knew. People would laugh, bound together by embarrassment, and the party would start again. With mild horror, she heard herself start a joke about three priests in a boat in front of all these people. She didn't often tell jokes. She wasn't sure she even understood this one. Once started, though, she staggered on through it, trying to remember the important details. The crowd listened to her, heads tilted, waiting in its judgment.

Just before the punch line a man interrupted her: "Anyone want another drink?" He rolled his hand out toward the kitchen. The crowd looked over at him.

Beryl stopped talking, the momentum lost. The women lowered their eyes in embarrassment.

Another man said, "Yes thanks."

Beryl waited for a moment, then tried to speak again.

The second man added, "Any dark beer."

Now a tall blond man leaned down in her direction and insisted that she tell the punch line. He apologized for the rudeness of his friends.

Beryl said, "No thanks." She knew it wouldn't work now. The man insisted. He put his hand on her shoulder. His eyes were earnest and determined; perhaps he thought he was being kind. She told the punch line. The humor was lost and only a few of the women laughed, out of pity.

She tried to imagine the three men in white fur suits trekking across the frozen sea, their rudeness as some age-old ritualized sparring for power. They were too noisy for a small cold cage on the tundra. They were too noisy even for this party. She felt sure that in the world of the future they would become extinct. Only those used to living on leftovers of one kind or another would survive in the future—women, the poor. Some in India might even flourish.

At the end of the party the blond man insisted on driving Beryl home. He said the streets and the subway were too dangerous at night for a woman alone. She accepted in the end because several people were watching them and smiling. He seemed to be friends with most of the people here, especially the women, whom he talked to easily, one hand frequently reaching out to touch their hands or hair. He had unusually wide cheekbones and green eyes. The women listened eagerly, smiling at his touch.

When he and Beryl reached his car parked on the street, he nodded toward it with implied modesty. Its hunched graceful curves gleamed with power and money. Beryl knew that although the car looked small, it was really just compact, like a black hole. If it could be dismantled properly and spread out, it would turn itself into a house with a lawn, or a mountain of food three buildings high. She knew that in the world of the future, there wouldn't be cars like this even in museums. There would be no private houses with lawns or pleasure vehicles. There would be only small groups of people dependent on one another for survival. There would be hard and constant work for food in a sick and plundered nature. These cars would exist only in photographs, along with the bears.

As he put the car into drive, Beryl heard the smooth clunk of the doors automatically locking. She looked at her door uneasily.

"Safety mechanism," he said as he accelerated out onto the street. "So neither of us falls out on the turns." He drove competently and too quickly as he chattered about his work in international banking. He frequently took his eyes away from the road to face Beryl as he spoke. When he did this, she found herself looking away from him and ahead to the road to watch for upcoming obstacles.

Parking in front of her house, he leaned over her more quickly than she'd thought possible. The air in the car contracted. She pressed back against the door. The car became a cage. He was so tall and hollow she had a momentary impression they could not be of the same species. No one watched them now and he regarded her intently with the sort of expression men wore when absorbed with fixing furniture or watching football. The kind of expression one had when alone. She thought she could try turning around to unlock the door, but she didn't want to have her back to him at all.

"Back off," she said. She startled herself at the clear depth of her voice.

He didn't seem to hear. He touched his hand to her face and said he felt honored being this close to such an untamed woman. She pulled her head back flat against the glass of the window. His hand followed.

She thought, An untamed woman. She said, "Get away."

His hand slid down her neck, his fingers slipped beneath her shirt at the collarbone. She was pressed sideways into the seat. She couldn't get any farther away. To her own surprise, she pulled her arm back and punched her fist into the hard bridge of his nose with a strength she'd always dreamed about releasing. Beneath her hand she felt a small click, like a light switch. Beneath her hand his mouth opened in a high thin shriek.

She unlocked the door, pulled it open and walked up the path to her home, where she paced shakily behind the locked door for an hour before she could sit down and look in disbelief at the hand that had committed such violence.

She needed to leave this place.

CHAPTER 7

On the bush plane from Winnipeg to Churchill, Manitoba, Beryl had a chance to get to know two members of the four-person expedition.

David Golding took the seat beside her. He was one of the best naturalist-cameramen, but he had also been picked for his size. He was only an inch taller than Beryl and just as thin. He wore a stylish leather jacket, which she thought not thick enough at all for where they were going. His features seemed slightly exaggerated, like a caricature—oversized nose, sharp and humorous eyes, the lips a thin clean line. She thought he looked like an elf who shopped in SoHo. When he'd introduced himself in the airport his voice boomed out much bigger than his small frame, like a radio announcer she'd seen on TV. She had felt some embarrassment for his rolling voice in the lounge. She could sense people turning around to look at her and the two men. Her own voice dwindled in response, and they'd had to ask her twice how the trip had been so far.

The second member of the team was the naturalist, Butler. He sat on the far side of David. He would advise them about the bears' behavior and write the article accompanying Beryl's pictures. He'd introduced himself only by his last name. Beryl guessed that his first name must be something effeminate, like Cecil or Francis. He wore the practical outdoor clothes of someone who wished for a short and common name with hard consonants, like Nick or Ted. Butler was tall and powerfully built and he kept getting up to stand restlessly in the aisle with his thumbs hooked into his back pockets and his pelvis tilted forward. He didn't hold on to anything for balance in the erratically bouncing plane. Beryl kept glancing forward to the pilot in the open cockpit to make sure he hadn't seen Butler ignoring the FASTEN SEATBELTS sign. She felt like she had in fifth grade watching her friends sneak cigarettes in the bathroom.

David wore a large watch that contained a glowing three-dimensional picture of an open eye. He noticed Beryl looking at it and boomed out, "Like the watch? It's a hologram of my own eye."

Butler glanced toward the watch from the corner of his eye, and Beryl's own mouth had probably opened a bit, for David laughed and reached forward to touch her arm. He said, "Sorry, I'm lying. I do it all the time. I got this watch for just that moment when people's eyes sneak down for a second look." She saw now that the hologram's eye was blue and his were brown. His touch on her arm felt warm and light but she sat back farther in her seat, for she could feel the push of his voice on her face and smell the cheese-dusted popcorn he'd been eating in the terminal. She sometimes wished she had ears like a cat so she could fold them back as cats did when people pushed their faces in too close.

He asked, "This your first expedition? You worried? My first was on piranhas, and on the plane ride down I kept examining each of my limbs and wondering how the prosthetics would look." He snorted.

She had seen a special on Madagascar that he'd worked on. At one point the camera had zoomed in all the way and followed an eagle hunting. She'd watched the flutter of the feathers across its neck, the strain in its shoulders, its cruel golden eyes. Each time the eagle dipped or turned, its leather-taloned feet kicking empty into the movement, the camera turned with it, not following, but moving in sync. She couldn't reconcile this noisy man beside her with the skill and instinct in that camera work.

"Filming the piranhas that time," he said, "I had to stay submerged in what was basically a clear plastic coffin. The camera stuck out into the water from one end. They wanted the box to be transparent so it wouldn't cast so many unattractive shadows on the little fishies. I had to lie in this thing underwater every day for two weeks, trying to focus through that brown slimy river. The box didn't work so well. I got wet. The camera got wet. Two Hitachis died before we just gave in and ordered straight underwater cameras." He held out an imaginary camera, peered down through it. "The tropics are amazing. Ever been down there?"

Beryl shook her head, but he kept talking so smoothly she guessed he hadn't really needed an answer. Behind David, she saw Butler sitting back down in his chair to stare out his window as though he weren't listening.

"Anything grows there. Anything, and quick. Plants, animals, fungi. Autogenesis is a fact of life. Even your lunch gets up and steps off the plate if you don't eat it fast enough. Lizards move so fast, it's unreal. Smooth as mammals. In the river, staying wet for so long, I grew this amazing orange aquatic mold in my hair, along the roots. As it got larger it looked just like a mutated rooster's crown. Had to keep my head shaved for three months." He made a smoothing motion over his head to show nothing there. "Hated it. With no hair, my nose stuck out even worse. I looked like a midget Kojak."

He looked sideways at her then. "Ah ha. Caught you. Looking at my schnoz. Fascinated, weren't you? Sort of squared-off, huh? Like a toaster oven. You were thinking 'toaster oven,' weren't you? Admit it."

She stared at him, beginning to smile.

"When the piranhas came, lots of them would appear all at once in the muck, just a few feet away. Moving quick, right for my face. Scared the shit out of me every time, until they bonked their little bodies up against the glass." He smiled wide and vicious. She laughed in surprise. He touched her again on the arm. "Hey, you've got a nice laugh," he said. His eyes were a sharp brown, the left one squinted permanently from the camera work. "I think I'll enjoy working with you. Though, God knows, you talk too much."

Beryl felt most people's touches as either overtly sexual or like small punches meant to keep her back. However, she didn't mind his touch at all. His hand rested dry and warm on her arm and she felt as though he knew how hard it had been this morning to say good-bye to her parents and get on the plane. Already, his voice did not bother her as much. She guessed he might be gay or had a wife whom he loved deeply.

"Look, don't you worry. The hardest thing for me to learn," he said, "was to keep quiet while the camera was rolling. Some of my best filming has my voice in the middle of it saying things like 'Shit, look at it go!' But you do still photography, so you've got it made." Although his face looked young, maybe early thirties, his hair was graying and his neck permanently hunched forward from leaning into the camera. He would also get into the cage.

After the first hour, David said, "Psst, hey Butler."

Butler looked over, standing again in the aisle.

"Why are you standing so much?" asked David.

Butler raised his eyebrows. "I don't like small seats, makes me nervous when you have to stay seated with everyone else sitting too. Makes my bones ache. At least once we get to Churchill I'll be out in the open, on my own feet." He held out his arms in the small plane as though taking in the vastness of the prairies. His right hand hit the overhead luggage rack.

Beryl asked if he'd been born in the country and he smiled and said, "No, lived my first fifteen years in Queens." David chortled and reached out to touch Butler's hip. Butler stepped back, then turned the movement into a quick drop down in his seat.

Later in the afternoon Butler shortened Beryl's name to Bear and laughed loudly at his own joke. It was with his mouth open laughing that Beryl first noticed how large and soft his lips were. Though the rest of his features were masculine—wide jaw, strong nose—he had thick and sensuous lips that reminded Beryl vaguely of Marilyn Monroe's. Mostly he kept pulling his mouth wide and tight in an effort to thin his lips. This habit gave his face a rather strained look, making him appear harsher than he might have otherwise.

David began to tell of the first time he'd filmed the manatees. "They look like someone crossed a walrus with Grandma Walton. Solid fat, big wet eyes. A crowd of them will hang in the water in front of you, heads up like they're standing. Actually, they all look just like my Aunt Amelia in her flannel nightgown—"

"Ha," said Butler. "Manatees are about as exciting as watching cows fart." He pulled his mouth wide again into a semblance of a grin.

David smiled politely. His hands stilled and returned to his lap. Butler looked up the aisle.

Beryl found herself looking from one to the other. She felt responsible for breaking the silence between them. She tried asking lightly how they'd gotten into this field.

David said, "Oh, I've known what my career would be ever since as a child I saw them filming an episode of Mutual of Omaha's 'Wild Kingdom.' I was raised in the city—punchball in the alleys, baseball in parking lots. I can't describe the awe I felt at the presence of those powerful, brave and silent men who knew the wilderness. My awe continued even after the grizzly bear that Jim had to wrestle was rolled onto the set on a dolly, doped out of its mind."

David imitated Marlin Perkins's slow and deliberate speech, as though he were always chewing on something leathery. David's mouth and eyes rolled energetically during his performance, and Beryl thought it wasn't so much an impersonation as an interpretation, a distillation of a character through David's habitual gestures and expressions. He clearly loved to perform.

Butler said that he'd had an older brother who used to take him on expeditions through the botanical gardens, where they would pretend they were Lewis and Clark trying to find the Pacific. Butler smiled to himself then and looked out one of the windows. Beryl noticed that he used the past tense in describing his brother. She felt David settle a little in his seat, but neither of them interrupted. Butler said that those times had been the best in his life. He'd decided on this line of work when he'd seen a beer commercial showing a film crew, after a hot tiring day of filming lions on the savannah, drinking beer and singing songs round a campfire. To him, this had looked a lot like what his brother would have chosen.

"Don't answer if you don't want to, but what happened to

your brother?" Beryl asked, her voice soft, expecting Butler to describe how he had been killed in a freak accident or by a wasting childhood disease. She could feel the comforting sad expression forming on her face already.

Butler looked at her and she could tell he thought she was prying. "He ran away," said Butler, "when he was fourteen. We haven't seen him since." He sat back down in his chair, looked out the plane window. She could see only the back of his head now, the pink hollow at the back of his ear. His voice continued more quietly, "His name was Stanley."

Beryl tried to imagine growing up thinking about a beloved older brother who had left her behind, who could return at any time. She saw the young Butler on the front lawn each day playing only the games he would want his brother to find him playing. She imagined Butler thinking each day that if he were just a bit better, more the way his brother would want, then his brother would return home. She saw him applying for this job.

Beryl asked the men if anyone had seen them off at the airport. She wanted to be asked the same question. She wanted to say she had a boyfriend who'd said good-bye to her. She would live with these men for a month and she didn't want any sexual tension. She had decided to name her boyfriend Max. Max sounded like the sort of name a long-term boyfriend should have. At home she'd left his name on the answering machine to scare off potential burglars.

David said a friend had kindly driven him in through

terrible traffic; Butler had driven himself. Neither of them asked her.

Beryl knew her life might depend on these two men. She talked with both in turn, listening carefully to their responses. She realized later that they'd discussed their lives only in the past, saying nothing of the expedition.

CHAPTER 8

Once they left Winnipeg behind they saw no more cities. After twenty minutes, there weren't even roads, houses, or cleared land. From the plane's window, she looked down at the passing scenery for a solid half hour and didn't see even a power line. She felt she'd traveled back two hundred years. She felt she'd traveled to a different planet. At three in the afternoon they left behind the trees. The land swept on below, flat, gray-green, covered with twisting rivers and lakes of a crystal blue untouched by even dirt, for the Arctic has no substance as complex as dirt, only rock and sand like a newborn world. To have soil, it would need tall trees, crawling worms, bacteria, decomposition. Three feet below the surface the ground is eternally frozen, summer and winter. Time paces differently. A single day can last two months, the sun making slow circles at the top of the sky, round and round like a hawk hunting. Spring and fall don't really exist. Summer is a fast and desperate lunge.

Beryl was stunned by the expanse of flat terrain without even hills or mountains as boundaries. In country like this, big creatures could survive, living free for their entire lives without knowing humans existed.

About midday she noticed a wide brown river, very different from the ice-water blue of the others. She touched David's arm and pointed down to the brown swath, asking the name of the river. He held up his finger for her to wait and stepped to the pilot. When David sat back down, the small bush plane began to descend with a speed that floated Beryl's stomach up near her lungs and pushed her back in her chair with queasiness. When they leveled off she looked cautiously out the window. They glided perhaps sixty feet from the ground.

After a moment she realized she was now looking at a river of caribou. Large deer with small antlers and young that trotted along beside, their heads held up. The caribou rolled on below like water, pouring and eddying. They moved on with the patient, mindless stride of the indomitable. She looked as far back and forward as she could within her flat airplane window and she could see no end, she could see no sides. She'd never seen this many animals together; she'd never seen this many humans together. The movement simply continued, rolling south across land that looked as if it couldn't sustain life any bigger than birds and small rodents. Not even trees could live this far north. And here were ten thousand caribou.

The pilot shut off the engine for a minute and they coasted in sudden whistling silence. David held up his finger and mouthed, "Listen." After a moment she could hear it over the sound of the wind, the subtle echoing clicks of their hooves on the rocks, the hollow booming cracks of their antlers colliding. She strained forward in her seat and listened to the engulfing sound of a species on the move through an area named the Barrens.

As they flew up farther across the tundra Beryl began to be aware of a lightening in the air outside the airplane's windows, a clarity. She learned later it was because there was less dust in the air up here, less moisture. As they moved north she began to see details of objects far away, as if she'd been living in a fog all her life and not known it. The outline of a distant lake resolved itself as clearly as in a dream, as though it were pressed right up against her eyes. When she looked around inside the plane, which had been closed since Winnipeg, her fellow passengers appeared darkened and slightly fuzzy.

The effect would intensify as winter approached. Already snow was forecast for the weekend. She looked back out the airplane window at this new planet.

At Churchill the final member of the group was late. None of them knew what Jean-Claude, the local guide, looked like, but he would be easy to spot; the airport was empty except for a candy machine and a folding table with tickets spread across it. Beryl, used to the mammoth gleaming airports of New York and Boston, stared at the plain plywood walls enclosing a space the size of a living room. The walls didn't even have windows, only a single large poster of a woman stepping out of the surf with HAWAII written across her wet T-shirt. Beryl saw Butler and David glance toward the poster and she watched their faces. David simply looked amused. Butler looked from the woman's face down her body as though she were a real person standing there.

"Jean-Claude's only twenty years old," said Butler while they waited, "but he's been guiding groups since he was fourteen. He's earned a lot of respect for his knowledge of navigation and the weather here, but his fame comes from his ability to survive bad situations. Unbelievable situations. Three years ago, one group—financed by some snowmobile company—wanted to cross Hudson Bay in the middle of winter for an ad to show the power of their machines.

"People who haven't been out in real arctic weather for a while just don't understand. Materials change. Metal can break off in your hand. Rubber and plastic crack. Even gas gets thick. It doesn't work so well. The moisture from your breath and sweat freezes instantly on clothes, hair, sleeping bags. There's no way to defrost the stuff and get the ice out. By the end of a long trip, your sleeping bag can weigh thirty pounds. To unfold it you have to jump on it to break the ice.

"These snowmobile guys had done all the experiments on their machines beforehand, all these laboratory tests, but they didn't understand the cold. No matter what space-age clothing you're wearing, you'll freeze to death sitting still on top of a machine."

David shivered. He touched his nose as though checking

for frostbite and said, "I hate the cold. I just fucking hate it."

Butler looked surprised. "The cold's great," he said. "It makes you feel stronger when you get back inside."

"Naw, it doesn't. I feel like a wet hanky. It gets into my bones. I really prefer assignments in the tropics. I only took this one 'cause they promised me Venezuela in January. Tree slug mating season. They grow to be monsters down there." He held out his hands to demonstrate. "They actually perform the nasty in midair, on this rope of slime hanging off a tree branch. With my luck the slime'll break and they'll land splat on me, still bopping away." He wrinkled up his face and rubbed his nose with the tips of his fingers. "But at least I'll come back with a tan."

Beryl watched the way Butler pulled his mouth thinner listening to David. She asked how people had gotten around in the Arctic with just dogs before.

"Oh," said Butler, "but it's much easier to get around with dog teams. With dogs you have to keep moving all the time to keep them going: cracking the whip, running alongside, balancing the sled, sometimes pulling right along with them. At night, even after moving all day, you have to run in a fast circle for twenty minutes slapping your gloves together just to get your hands working well enough to set up your tent, to light the fire, to warm your food and unfreeze your water. It's the strangest thing, cold like that. It works on you slow. Your body just won't do the simplest tasks."

"Look," said David. "I'm going over here to this poster to

look at this woman baking in the tropical sun on the beach. I'm going to channel my thoughts toward warmth and sun-tans and when you two have finished this discussion, you can call me over." David walked to the poster and began to search his pockets for change for the candy machine.

Beryl noticed Butler watching the poster woman's wet breasts as though they were going to do something interest-ing. "What happened to the snowmobile group?" she asked. He turned his head back to look at her.

"The snowmobiles died the second day. They were two hundred miles from Churchill. Without the machines, they couldn't pull all the food and shelter they needed. Jean-Claude got three of the five of them out alive."

A small man stepped in the door, closed it behind him. David walked back from the candy machine. The man paced toward the three of them with his hand held out. He walked in a painful and methodical way, something wrong with his right hip, a slight stiffness. Beryl knew just from looking that he'd left several bad situations by walking exactly that way for many many miles. He'd outlived even the sled dogs.

She would never have guessed he was only twenty years old. The harshness of the short but constant summer sun had bleached his eyebrows a pure white. His face moved stiffly as the faces of older people who have lived by the sea their entire lives. His skin blushed a slow pink except for three white spots on his cheeks the size of quarters. The pinker the rest of his features became, the more dead white the spots seemed. She realized they were caused by frostbite. She did not know if the blush came from the heat of the room or from having to greet them.

He took her hand. She felt a dry roughened palm like the raspy skin on the paw of a dog. She knew her own hand must feel soft and weak in comparison. His eyes rested on her, blue and level. She knew he was wondering how she would react if things went bad, if she would survive. He let go of her hand and shook hands with the others. Beryl wondered what he saw. Jean-Claude nodded, picked up some of their luggage and led the way toward the door. Beryl watched the men follow him. David tried to zip the front of his thin jacket while carrying two bags. The bags bumped him in the chest. He settled his face farther into the jacket's neck.

Butler yawned and stretched his long arms until his back cracked. Then he grabbed three bags and sauntered out the door into the open.

Beryl touched the palm of the hand that had shaken Jean-Claude's. Her hand felt soft, with the smooth fingers of a monkey. She could smell the clear air outside now and she felt something loosen inside her. She picked up her own bags and stepped toward the door.

Beryl guessed the temperature outside the terminal was in the low thirties, Fahrenheit. The wind blew about them like the wind she knew. It smelled of the sea, of salt. The air was like what she'd been used to breathing. The cold felt manageable. In the dark, in the car she could sense nothing of Churchill except that the road was very rough and there were no lights of houses visible until they were a hundred yards from the hotel. The hotel had a worn red carpet and a stuffed moose in the hall.

That night as she slept she confused the sheets of the bed with the white arms of a gigantic bear who waltzed her gently across the rolling flat plains of the tundra.

CHAPTER 9

In the morning, she went outside and stood in the parking lot of the hotel. All her life she'd lived where the landscape rose taller than she, cutting off her vision. She'd lived among houses and vacationed in the mountains. She'd driven along roads lined with trees. Here, the land rolled out flat. There were no trees. No buildings outside of town, no fences or power lines, no hedges or long waving grass to distract from the utterly flat line of the land pulling the eye out to the horizon. Most of the lichen and tundra vegetation stood no taller than a well-trimmed lawn. Except for the buildings, she could have been standing in the center of a golf course as wide as China. The clarity of the air hurt her eyes. The smooth horizon didn't grow blue and hazy with distance. She wondered how far away the horizon was. She felt as if her eyes couldn't quite focus.

The sky above soared open, clear and heavy with light for

the complete circle above her head. The sky was a presence, a startling bright Bermuda-water blue. It stretched bigger by far than anything she'd ever seen. The sky dwarfed the land in size and color and depth. In order to live in this world, Beryl knew she would have to resist the vast width of the sky and remember which part of the world she inhabited.

The town itself huddled against the ground. The one- or two-story prefab houses were all painted in dismal gray, beige and white. They had small windows. The parking lot was dirt. The concrete road heaved with cracks and bumps from winter. In front of the houses were parked pickup trucks and jeeps, vehicles that could drive on these roads and on the tracks past the airport and the town dump. No highways led out of town, for there was no place to drive to. The backyards of the last houses merged with the tundra that rolled outward, uninterrupted for five hundred miles. Everything from cars and fruit to vinyl siding and alcohol was brought in by plane or train. The town earned its income from fish and tourism.

Beryl thought that the buildings drained the surrounding scenery of beauty and balance. The dull colors, the dirt streets, the broken and heaving concrete. On the far side she could see boulders and then the road leading to the town dump, the sea open and gray beyond.

From the start of summer until the sea freezes again sometime in November, there isn't much for the bears to eat. They prefer to eat seal, are designed to hunt seal from the top of the ice. During the summer, when the ocean has melted, the bears lose up to one-third of their body weight.

Forty miles to the east of Churchill is Cape Churchill. The sea off the cape freezes the earliest of any place on Hudson Bay because of the fresh water pouring into the bay from the Churchill River. In October the bears begin to arrive in the area around Churchill in greater and greater numbers, waiting patiently without food through the months of October and November. They break into deserted cabins and haunt the town dump, licking the insides of old peanut butter jars clean with delicate black tongues. Then wander heavy and ghostlike through the streets of the town at midnight, chuffing thoughtfully to themselves like people with things on their minds. The moment the ice is strong enough to support their weight, they stalk off across it far from humans to their winter hunting grounds, to the frozen ocean and warm seals.

The bears don't respond predictably to people. Sometimes they run away, short tails flicking up in alarm. Sometimes they step forward, swinging their heads from side to side, sniffing. Sometimes they seek out and stalk humans, drifting behind them silent and white.

The townspeople keep their children and animals inside. Their houses have boarded-up windows, peepholes in doors, back steps with nails and cut glass sprinkled across them. They have a patrol car just for the polar bears. It cruises about at night with searchlights on the top, sirens, infrared binoculars.

When Beryl arrived, no humans had been killed by bears for three years. The townspeople repeated the fact with pride. They valued their tourist trade. Every visitor during October and November went out to the town dump in closed cars to watch the polar bears eat garbage.

The expedition began at the town dump. They would be staying for a week in Churchill to get pictures of the bears who lived on the garbage there. The morning after the team arrived, they drove out in a little Japanese van with a sunroof and no windows along the sides. Already five or six cars were parked by the garbage, no one dumping anything. People in the cars drank coffee and waited, watching for the bears, their windows closed tight. David stood up as soon as the van stopped, got his camera out and began to crank the handle to open the sunroof.

Beryl felt surprise, but said nothing. Here there would be no cage around them. The other two men weren't even looking out the windows for bears. They were pulling out the coffee thermos and donuts. Cautiously, she peered out the front and back windows. Nothing to see but garbage, stripped bodies of cars, old fridges, sea gulls pecking. David stuck his head and camera out of the roof.

He quickly jerked back inside. "You know, I hate when people throw away perfectly good couches. This one's even a sleeper." He saw her expression, smiled over at her. "Come on up," he boomed. "No bears in sight."

She collected her camera and film and slowly stood up next to him, putting her head out of the hole. She looked around. The garbage lay in piles all about like hills. She didn't know if she could capture the clarity of the air on film. She found herself staring up at the sky. It shone as blue and hard as a lid. She thought if she had a long enough arm she could reach up and push that arctic sky off and behind would be her own sky, cloudy, soft and insubstantial.

David was filming already. He moved quietly and carefully, his body twisting around as smoothly as a camera dolly, panning across the garbage. His face hung motionless behind the camera, blank. The only tension showed in his left eye, which he squinched closed to see better out the right. As she looked at him now she couldn't imagine him talking loudly in his booming voice or caring about others as he touched their hands.

A car tire burned hazy black smoke off to her left. She began to photograph the people waiting in the cars. At first they looked curiously at her and David, then they lost interest. She assumed that a lot of camera crews came up here. At the hotel this morning she'd seen a small notice board with WELCOME NATURAL PHOTOGRAPHY TEAM on it, their names spelled out below. Butler still didn't have a first name. She wondered if he'd told the hotel staff to write it that way or if he'd crept down last night under the cover of darkness and popped out the letters of his first name one by one.

Her name on a public board startled her. She hadn't yet realized what a small town this was. One thousand people lived in Churchill, the largest human outpost for several hundred miles. It took such effort to live here. In the winter people kept engine block heaters plugged into outlets so the cars would start. The small town was perched on the sea; everything in it smelled of salt.

She was getting some good background pictures in spite of the awkwardness of the gloves she had to wear against the cold. The people all looked off slightly to the left. They talked, sipped coffee and ignored her.

As Beryl shifted the camera, she saw something white to the left of her. She thought it was a refrigerator. She continued to snap photos. After another three pictures, she realized the people were watching the fridge. She turned toward it. Two yards away from her stood a large white bear. Even with the two feet of van added to her own height, the bear towered over her. She'd never seen such a large animal so close. It breathed her smell in, no noise, but she saw its nostrils open and its chest expand. She felt her mind still like the water of a pond.

She remembered her dream, dove down into the van, hitting the back of David's knees and taking him with her. His camera cracked against the roof as it came through. Looking up she saw a large paw questing about the hole in the roof, black pads, yellow nails. Claws scratched against the metal of the van. From the front seat Butler and Jean-Claude looked back dumbfounded, still holding their coffee.

Beryl jumped up and, keeping her head back, turned the little handle to close the roof. From the half-closed sunroof she heard her first polar bear sound, a small irritated chuff. Then the muffled *whump* of weight hit the side of the van, knocking Beryl down. She watched out the windshield as the bear stalked slowly away with the fat-bottomed pride of a senator. People in the other cars were laughing.

In that first moment as Beryl had faced the bear, she'd thought it was going to move its paw toward her and they would again begin to dance.

"Shit shit shit," David said as the bear walked away. "I didn't get it on film." He ran to the front of the van and filmed what he could of the bear's retreat.

Butler began to guess excitedly at the bear's size. He offered out each of the numbers with pride and possession, as though in guessing the animal's height or weight, he laid claim to it. "Standing—nine feet tall," he said. "A thousand pounds. Paws—twelve inches wide. Medium-size one."

Jean-Claude kept his face turned from the rest of the group while they talked about the bear. So far he hadn't talked much with any of them. He looked out over the trash in the direction the bear had gone, to where the tundra ran, interrupted only by oceans, for the width of the world.

CHAPTER 10

That second night in the Arctic Beryl dreamed again of the bear. This time they were sitting across from each other at a candlelit table where two large silver domes covered the plates in front of them. Beryl's date sat with the natural grace of the active. His fur gleamed with health. His body was too large for the table and his legs and feet pressed over into her side of the table. She tried to keep her feet decorously tucked under her chair, but he needed even that area, and his heavy weight leaned against her no matter which way she moved. She pitied him for the depths of his need. She wondered if he would be offended if she removed her plate from the table and ate her food off the ground. His black nose wrinkled slightly at the smell of the food, and the corners of his mouth were wet. The waiter's hands reached smoothly forward to pull the covers off the food.

·　·　·

The next day they saw thirteen bears. The garbage dump was thirty miles from where the animals gathered in greatest density, and Beryl knew that their migration to this area had only begun. The bears would continue to arrive for another month. Still, at least one bear was visible at all times, snuffling through the garbage, gnawing on a tire or walking purposefully toward the van.

The bears seemed to be willing to give anything a try as food, eating the foam rubber out of couches, tugging the seats off snowmobiles, chewing on vinyl car roofs. Standing up in the van Beryl saw one bear sniffing a closed can of paint, putting his teeth to each edge, curling his lips back, then turning the can over to try again. Each time the bears found something they considered edible, they looked content, chewing hard, strings of drool rolling from their mouths.

One bear found a deflated plastic clown with a bell in the bottom, the type little kids punch. Each time the bear chewed on it, the bell rattled. The bear swiveled her ears toward the bell, slapped at it halfheartedly with a paw. Beryl dropped her head back down through the sunroof, told Jean-Claude to drive closer, to a spot up sun of the bear.

As she zoomed in on the bear's half-closed eyes and exposed black lips, the bear chewed gingerly through the clown's red button vest. The plastic squeaked.

Butler spoke from the front of the van. "Up here in the Arctic there's almost nothing that's naturally poisonous. The plants are all edible. No poisonous snakes or insects. Polar bears are born curious. No caution in them. They explore just about anything new, chew on it. With humans, this hasn't worked so well. The bears'll seek out each new garbage dump, campsite and oil rig. Sniff all around, lap up some antifreeze. Get shot out of fear."

David and Beryl quickly worked out their bear watches. Only one of them filmed or photographed at a time. The other swiveled about in the small sunroof, steering clear of the lenses, staying watchful. They were constantly pressed up against each other, either back to back or front to back. They moved their legs in unison.

Pressed against him, Beryl felt the way he worked with the camera, the way he braced his legs, shifted his weight, focused, the silent vibration of the camera pressed against both of them. She saw firsthand his ability to predict which direction a bear was going to turn, while she, who was able to see outside of the limiting focus of the lens, wasn't able to guess at all. Once, when he had followed the leisurely, rambling path of a young bear for over twenty minutes without making a mistake, she'd turned to look at his face and saw his lip lifted in concentration, the sharp whiteness of his teeth gleaming below.

When David saw it was time to retreat, he would cradle her shoulder, push gently down. She responded immediately. During her turn to warn, she pulled gently on his sleeve. They descended smoothly. By the end of the day, she understood that he was probably gay. She had no more problem leaning up against him than she did against her mother.

Each time they left the sunroof, they sank as one creature, winding the top quickly shut after them. They would hear from outside a snuffling above or below, the rasp of hair coarse as a brush against the metal of the van, a thumping against the side. They would wait. Whenever a bear began to approach the front or back windows, Jean-Claude would turn the car on, shift the gears to reverse or forward as needed. He would hold the brake delicately down as they all looked through a thin sheet of glass at the creature padding forward.

The bear would approach slowly, its wide back swaying. About ten feet away it would push upright, its long neck and head rising higher than their van, its belly spread broad and strong. The bear would stand in front of them, sniffing, uncertain, then step closer, holding a single clawed paw out for balance. The van would roar in reverse. They would all laugh nervously while Jean-Claude circled the vehicle around, moving to another spot.

Each time a bear stepped in closer, Beryl imagined it charging forward, Jean-Claude frantically stepping on the gas, the van rocking backward, the bear running faster, the glass breaking, cold air suddenly in the van, blood on Jean-Claude and Butler. Jean-Claude trying to get out of his seat, the bear reaching in . . .

Driving back into town for lunch, Beryl asked David why Jean-Claude allowed the bears to get so close to the van.

"Oh," said David. "It's the same as safaris in Africa. There the tops of the jeeps are open. I mean right on open, not even a screen, so everyone can stick their heads and cameras out of the van and lean over the side to take pictures of the lion or cheetah taking a nap five feet away. And I mean literally five feet away. Conceivably any lion could just hop right into that hole, make scrambled eggs of everyone inside and no one could do a thing. But it never happens. The lions aren't quite sure what they want to do. Contrary to popular belief, humans aren't high on their list of edibles. They'd rather chomp on an antelope. They're confused by the jeep's smell and metal exterior. So enough time passes and the lions get used to the jeeps. They get used to cameras, to the smell of mint deodorant, to Kansas accents rolling across the savannah saying, 'Oh, isn't she pwetty!'"

Beryl looked over her shoulder at the dump. She could still see a young bear rolled onto her back, staring up at the sky, chewing thoughtfully on a hiking boot.

During lunch back at the hotel, Butler made a number of jokes about how well David was getting to know Beryl.

"Hey, David," Butler said. "You get tired of guarding Beryl in that tiny little sunroof, I'll take your place." He made some clicking noises to show enjoyment. Butler smiled at Beryl as he said it, his thick lips curved. He didn't seem tense or embarrassed. He seemed to think she'd enjoy the joke as much as any of them, perhaps even more.

Butler wore cologne. He smelled all the time of sweet musk and heat. He wore his shirtsleeves rolled back on his flat large forearms. Beryl's forearms were freckled, golden-haired and thin. At one time she'd worked seriously at weightlifting, but although she'd doubled the amount of weight she could handle, her arms only looked longer and more sinewy. The glistening heavy men in the health club could bench-press three times her body weight with sharp grunts of satisfaction. She'd moved about them with a constant sense of fear. Once one of them stepped backward laughing at a joke and slapped her hard into the cold metal web of a Nautilus machine. The man moved away and apologized but Beryl had still felt a hot flush covering her neck and arms. If Beryl and Butler had stood back to back, the top of her head would nestle neatly into the hollow between his shoulder blades.

Beryl looked at the other men for their response to Butler's joke. She'd be spending a month with them. She tried to look impassive. David looked uncomfortable. Butler laughed hard enough for them all. For a moment Jean-Claude looked away from the tundra to Beryl. In his brief glance she felt a connection, a message passed that she couldn't yet understand. Then he turned back, scanning for bears. His hands lay loose on the steering wheel. They hadn't let go the entire day.

Butler laughed awhile longer. He had one of those complete laughs that Beryl normally liked. The skin of his forehead rolled back as though he were surprised, his eyes opened and then his chest and shoulders began to shake up and down. He laughed like a young muscular Santa Claus. Beryl imagined him laughing like that and a girlfriend leaning up tight against him, blissful, shaking with his movement. Beryl hoped her own life would never depend on his judgment.

. . .

That afternoon it started to snow. The flakes fell thick and wet, covering the garbage of the dump with a pure layer of white. The bears moved through the snow, white on white. She saw them for the first time against a background other than old couches and broken glass. They merged into the blank beauty so that only the black triangles of their noses showed, their dark eyes. The snow muffled all sound except the wet squeaks beneath the pads of their feet and their heavy snorts as they stuck their snouts deep into the snow and sniffed for the scent of food.

When it got dark Jean-Claude drove them back to the hotel. Beryl sat by the window of her room watching the flakes twinkle down by the hotel's spotlight. The snow flattened everything. It erased the cars, the road and the mailboxes. Houses became magical palaces of sugar and ice. She had always imagined the North Pole this way, only there would have also been elves working cheerfully and flying reindeer pawing restlessly in their stalls.

A car turned the corner, drove slow and cautious down the street. The polar bear police car. It had two spotlights and a siren on the roof. The spotlights circled patiently across the snow.

The next day the gleaming snow covered everything and danced in the wind, shimmering pure in the sun and thin air. The sky above glittered with the light hard blue of thick glass. That evening when she came in from staring out at the snow and bears, her eyes hurt, a slow headache built up from the base of her skull. She had a hard time adjusting to the relative darkness of the hotel and grazed her hand along the faded velvet of the wallpaper as she walked slowly up to her room.

In the sun the colors of the snow and the bears and the sky reminded Beryl of when she used to get bad fevers as a child. Her temperature would frequently go up to a hundred and five or six. She would pant, her upper lip sticky with the sweat of her effort, her mouth open for her thick tongue. Her parents would take her to the hospital, stand about her bed and hold her hand. They stared in fascination at her pale face with its bright red spot of color on each cheek. She knew each time it happened that they thought once again how unwise they'd been to have a child this late in their lives. They didn't have the strength to deal with these unexpected events.

After a few times watching their worry, when she got a fever she would take the thermometer out of her mouth whenever they looked away. When they began to look back, she would slip it quickly back in, keeping her tongue away from it, holding it tight between her cool teeth. Each time they asked her, she'd smile and say she was feeling better, she would get up soon.

Once when she was seven the fever had been worse than ever, but by then she'd gotten better at pretending. Her parents had still looked worried but hadn't taken her to the hospital. When Beryl moved her head on the pillowcase the rasp of its material had filled her head. Each thread had crackled and snapped in her ear so harshly she wanted to scream. The slow drip of mucus down her throat kept her awake with its insidious slide. The room glittered. The illness was bad. It was very bad and it got worse during the night. The room seemed to be lit even though it was dark. The air seemed bright and warm and stuffy.

She could see her Raggedy Anne doll perfectly on the chair by the far wall. They looked at each other, eyes open and shining with fever. Beryl's skin stretched tight with heat and fatigue. She wanted to close her eyes. Her head slowly rolled over to the side, her eyes still open, and she could feel a hum beginning in her body, a vibration as subtle as that of light. It was then that she saw from the corner of her eye the fingernail on her left pinky. A single white cloud floated halfway up its clear pink length. The cloud was as light and fluffy as an early Sunday morning and just above it was the clear half-moon of the nail's growing edge, smooth and thin as milky ice. The precision of its curve startled her. She wanted to skate along its cool surface, its smooth moon edge. She wanted to exhale white clouds into its chill night air. She wanted to hear the sharp metal of skates on ice, feel the slight tremor in her ankles, float forward fast and cool. Looking at the cloud on her nail she knew what the world would be like if the sky were pink and sunsets blue. Looking at her nail and its one white cloud, she forgot her tiredness for a while and wasn't even sure when the vibration receded.

• • •

The third day at the dump they saw a young bear catch on fire. A mattress burned about twenty feet from the van. Beryl knew polar bears had no instinctive fear of fire for there were no fires out on the wet tundra or on the ice. Bears had been known to step right onto a campfire and stand still for a moment before confusion registered on their faces. The young bear lay quite close to the flaming mattress, black tongue neatly licking the mayonnaise out of an open jar that had been lobbed to her from a car. The bears craved fat, and mayonnaise contained lots of it, but the jars baffled creatures who were used to flesh. Their paws couldn't grip the glass, their tongues couldn't quite reach the bottom. They played with the jars, fascinated, frustrated, for hours.

The bear discovered she could control the slippery jar if she used all four paws. As she tried to get to the bottom she rolled slowly backward onto her shoulders, and onto the burning mattress. After a slow moment, Beryl thought nothing would happen, that it would be all right. Then the bear twitched her shoulder. She jumped up, shaking her back violently. Her left shoulder was on fire. She bit at it. Her muzzle started to burn. The fire moved across her face, across her shoulder. She threw her head up in the air. The flames burned faster. The fire moved down her back. She ran away, breathing hoarsely, the wind speeding the flames. They could smell burnt hair and flesh.

The bear ran over the ridge. David turned off his camera.

• • •

Beryl had begun to get used to the bears' bodies and sounds and smells: the waddle of their rears, the shorter fronts ready to charge, the wet snuffling breath. They had a meaty warm smell like an oversized cat. They ambled forward as though they had all the time in the world. The sounds of guns didn't scare them, for they were used to the much louder crack of sea ice beneath them. They had no natural fear of humans. Even packs of sled dogs didn't frighten them. The bears simply stepped forward, eyes moving, picking out their first victim.

At the end of the next week the expedition would move out forty miles to the northeast where the bears gathered in greater numbers and Beryl would get into her cage for the first time. The three men and she would spend almost a month out there, sleeping and eating together in a single bus, returning to Churchill only for the weekends.

Of the three others, Jean-Claude was the only one who still seemed an unknown. She knew little more about him than she'd learned that first day, except that she'd observed some of his habits. He sat very still during the long days in the van. Unlike most people, each of his movements had a reason: to turn up the heat, to shift the car into reverse, to adjust the rearview mirror for a better view of a bear. Otherwise he sat still, his hands on the wheel. He watched the others with a flat blue gaze. When he spoke his voice was quiet, almost a whisper, as though something might be startled if he talked any louder. He wore a loose gray turtleneck and jeans every day. She wondered if they were the same set, but she couldn't tell. His cheekbones were wide, his hair long, the back of his hands ridged with white tendons. He liked a lot of butter on his toast.

During breakfast one morning while they waited for David and Butler to join them, she tried to get him to talk. She asked him how cold it got during the winter.

He did not look at her while he answered. Instead he kept partly turned away, giving her only a profile. He stared at the wall on the other side of the room and answered her question in as few words as possible. "Negative sixty," he said.

"Wow," she replied. "I can't even imagine that. Once it got down to ten below in Boston, but I think that was counting the windchill factor." She smiled at him, trying for eye contact. He looked over at her for one moment, then away. She wondered if he was very farsighted from staring out across such large spaces so much of his life. She wondered if he was shy around women. "What's spring like?"

He spoke after a moment. "Fast. Lots of water."

She noticed the seriousness with which he thought out his words, as though he were communicating through Morse code and each additional letter was an effort. She started to smile. "You know, something that's always fascinated me are the muskox. Their hair is amazing, but I sometimes wonder with all those dreadlocks if there's anything much underneath. Like sometimes when you give a fluffy cat a bath and wet it's just a skinny little thing." She picked up her toast, took a bite. "Anyone ever shave them?"

She couldn't tell if he knew she was joking. His mouth was

a little twisted on one side, but that could be a smile or just tension at having to speak this much. In answer he simply shook his head, turning back to look at the far wall.

"How big are they really?" she asked.

"Big as the bears." He touched two fingers to his nose. "Their breath's noisy."

"You've been close enough to hear that?"

"Yes."

She gave up. She knew him no better than before. She thought asking him questions made him nervous, although he never fidgeted or tried to cut the conversation short. Instead he sat still, waiting for her questions to end.

She could imagine him doing almost anything. Baying suddenly deep and wild as a wolf, or leaving them two weeks into the expedition, simply walking off across the snow heading due north.

Beryl also asked Butler about the springtime. He had spent several years up here, working on different projects for *Natural Photography* or the Canadian government. He told her about spring while sitting next to her at lunch. He tended to lean in close when he spoke to her, much closer than he did to Jean-Claude or David. She didn't know if he was attracted to her or if this was just the way he talked to women. She found herself leaning backward, giving ground. He exuded a warm heat and breathed through his nose with an audible whisper. Even his face was larger than her's. On her it would have stretched almost down to the base of her neck.

Butler said, "Spring comes fast and noisy. There isn't much

time for it to get to summer. The temperature suddenly rises into the fifties and the sun shines. The snow melts all at once. The ground never thaws more than a few feet deep, even in the middle of summer, so the water has nowhere to go except into the harbor. It backs up on the unmelted harbor ice."

Beryl imagined the water weighing down the still frozen sea ice, building up slowly over the pier back to the first house and then to the second, flooding through the town and forming a thin milky skin in the night as smooth and perfect as glass, shattering each morning with the first door that opened. The waves moved out from that first door, broken ice tinkling outward across the town.

Butler said, inching even closer to Beryl, "The whole town is flooded. The weather's already hot. People wear T-shirts with thick winter pants and boots for sloshing through the water. Then one day the ice in the harbor finally cracks. It booms loud as guns. The water runs into the sea, the town's drained, and the next day the ground is dry and warm."

Beryl leaned back full against the booth, her head tucked into her neck in an effort to move back from Butler's face. David, she noticed, was staring down at his soup, stirring it. Jean-Claude watched her and Butler, motionless, one hand holding out a piece of toast, the blush rising to his cheeks again.

After a moment, Butler shifted a little away.

Beryl knew a spring only a week long would surprise her so much she wouldn't be able to sleep. She would stay up listening to the groaning of the ice, the high-pitched keening of tension as though through a boat's hull ten miles wide, the sharp clanks like metal against metal, the gentle crinkling of water on her doormat.

She imagined Butler on the day after the ice broke, standing in the center of a dry warm town, thankful the strange spring had passed.

CHAPTER II

That weekend the temperature plummeted. Three more inches of granulated snow fell overnight and Beryl went for a walk in the half-light of early morning through the still-falling snow. She needed some exercise and wanted to test out her new *Natural Photography* parka. She wanted to get away from the others for the first time in a week. A month ago, the temperature had hit the seventies; now, walking across town in the early morning, the air was so cold the snow squeaked like Styrofoam beneath her feet. The streets were deserted except for occasional cars that rolled by with steamed windows, blurred warm faces inside. Several people in the cars stared at her. She met no one else walking.

She walked quickly, trying to make a wide circle through the unfamiliar streets. Her ears filled with the sounds of her own breath and the slide of the parka's cloth against itself. Within five minutes of walking she unzipped the front and pulled down the hood. She'd been told sweat was the easiest way to die up here. Sweat would freeze quickly against the skin, cooling her body more rapidly than it could tolerate.

With the hood down she could see and hear so much more. She looked about easily, exhilarated to be the only human walking outside in the snowstorm. She looked through a window into a warmly lit room. A man in a bathrobe shuffled by in his bare feet. Snow fell between them. Beryl felt prepared, self-reliant, a wild creature.

A police car drove up from nowhere. It skidded to a stop in front of her, bumping half up on the sidewalk. The woman inside thrust open the passenger door.

"Get in," she said. "It's behind you."

Beryl turned to look over her shoulder.

The bear followed only thirty feet away. It came slowly to a halt when Beryl closed the car door after her. It turned its heavy face about, then wandered away down a driveway.

Beryl looked down at her gloves and saw that her hands had curled into themselves. In her dreams she'd been much closer to the bear than that. In her dreams she'd felt the area much more clearly, the open space limitless in all but one direction.

Beryl watched the bear disappear around a building and then looked toward the woman who had rescued her. Beryl assumed she'd be yelled at. She noticed her breath slowing down as though the danger had started only now.

The thin black woman wore a uniform with polar bear insignias on the shoulders. She said, "That was a really stupid thing to do." She glanced in the rearview mirror. "Actually, I think that was the *stupidest* thing I've *ever* seen a tourist do in my entire seven years in this town. And it's not like tourists are known for their smarts."

The woman spoke with a slight smile that made Beryl unsure whether or not she was supposed to smile back. Beryl assumed the officer was seriously angry, that she might even tell the magazine and they wouldn't let Beryl go out to the cage to sit among the bears. Panic filled her chest as it had when she was a child and her parents caught her disobeying. When they were mad they denied it, but their hands would shake and they used more force than needed to cut the bread or to brake the car so that everyone inside rocked back and forth with their emotion and the silence was stiff as the white in their eyes.

"Hi," the woman said, "I'm Margaret Johnson. What's your name?"

Beryl looked at her hands again. "Beryl Findham," she said.

"I'm the polar bear watch. You can call me Maggie." She drove back out onto the street and added, "Actually I lied just now. The stupidest thing was this tourist out at the dump— not a young boy either, but a man who had survived to his early thirties. He rolled down his window to pat the head of a bear. Now *that's* stupid." Maggie glanced over at Beryl, then turned to look again. "You OK? Don't feel light-headed do you? Where you from? How on earth did you survive this long with the brains of a turkey? Jesus, you're pale. You going to be sick?"

Maggie pulled the car over to the side of the road. She turned to Beryl. "You going into shock? Look at me."

Beryl looked.

"Open your eyes. Wider."

Beryl opened her eyes as wide as they would go.

"I think they're dilated. Breathe. Don't forget to breathe. It's important. Look, don't you go schizo on me, not while you're in my car. And don't you vomit. I'm not cleaning that up. Look at me." Maggie grabbed Beryl by the ears. She shook her hard three times and screamed into her face. "Wake the fuck up! You're fine now."

Beryl stared at her in amazement.

Maggie asked, "What year is it?"

"Nineteen ninety-four," Beryl said.

"Who's the U.S. president?"

"Clinton."

Maggie sat back. "OK, I guess you're fine. Sorry." She started the car and drove out onto the street. "They train us to do things like that. They say to get your attention. Focus you on something other than fear. First time I've had a chance to try it. Did that hurt?"

Beryl grinned. "Yeah, quite a bit. I think I heard something crack."

"Really?" The right side of Maggie's mouth jerked up. "Sorry. At least you don't look like curdled milk anymore."

Beryl found her hands slowly uncurling and she took off her mittens to look at them curiously. She felt the width of her smile. "I'm the photographer for the *Natural Photography* team here in town. I'm from Boston." Beryl listened to the words. No hesitation. "Boston, Massachusetts," she added.

Maggie nodded. "I've heard of it. I'm from Atlanta, but I hate the heat more than anything." She looked off to the left quickly, but Beryl saw that it was only a snow-covered car. "I've always figured there's only so much you can sweat, but you can always put on more clothing."

Beryl laughed at that and saw with surprise the small shyness of Maggie's smile.

"No, really," Maggie continued, "I like the cold. I eat more up here and my body heats up. In Atlanta I was always feeling a little sickly, like I couldn't breathe in all the way. Here I can breathe." She tapped herself in the chest with her fist. "You sure your ears are all right? Is there anything that can be hurt there? Some sort of important muscle or something? Look, it's not my fault. They said to shock you out of it. Your ears just looked handy."

Beryl nodded and touched her ears. They felt hot.

"I also moved up here for my kids. I want them to grow up where there's enough room to play."

The frozen plains spread out from them in every direction. Beryl laughed. This time Maggie looked surprised that she had said something funny. Beryl realized she hadn't laughed much since this trip had started.

They continued to talk together until the sun rose and Maggie's watch was over. They went into the hotel for breakfast. Maggie had a huge meal: waffles, eggs, Cream of Wheat.

"It's not only the cold," she said. "It's terror. I see just one of those things moving through the night, big as a goddamn boat, and these pancakes are completely gone." She patted her belly and snorted. She was a stringy woman, the kind who was always eating Yodels and Snickers and moving quickly, heat pouring off her. "In Atlanta, the biggest, scariest thing I ever saw were Dobermans, and they only weigh eighty pounds."

"How'd you get this job?" Beryl asked.

"Oh, they had signs up about it for months. No one wanted it. Not out all night in the cold, not looking for hungry polar bears. But I wanted it. I needed it. Money, you know. They wouldn't let me take it at first. I'm a woman, hmm, and black." Maggie looked straight at Beryl for a second, and Beryl wasn't sure exactly what her face should be showing. "It's not like they said anything about the black part, but they talked a lot about the woman part, me being weaker and stuff. Like the biggest beefed-up man would be able to take a polar bear charge any better than little old me. Also, the town still thought of me as a tourist, practically from the tropics. I mean, I'd been here a whole year by then but they still figured every day would be the last straw, that I'd pack up and go."

Maggie rubbed her thumb slowly around the lip of her coffee mug. "Then this kid got mauled out in the rocks by the beach. Mauled bad, the skull cracked before the bear lost interest. The kid's head was in the bear's mouth, kid screaming, when it just spat him out and walked off. Kid lived, but he lost his sense of balance. His legs are perfectly fine, but you stand him upright and he falls over like the room tilted."

Maggie let go of the cup, put both hands in her lap. "So after that they hired me. I like the job. These two months each year are a kind of vacation to me. My husband, Gerry, has been gone six years now, back down south. Couldn't deal with things up here. The one winter he spent here, he practically lived in the fireplace." Maggie smiled, looked away. "These two months pay for all the extras the kids and I need for the rest of the year, the things I can't handle being just a mail carrier. For these two months the kids stay at the neighbor's. I live alone in the car. I carry a gun, wear a uniform. I'm tough. For two months I'm no mother. I'm fucking Dirty Harry. You know, it's different."

Maggie and Beryl agreed to meet that night so Beryl could photograph a night watch. Beryl didn't tell anyone else on the team. She left dinner early, put on her warmest clothes. Maggie told her it got cold sitting still in the car all night. Beryl snuck out the back of the hotel.

She stepped out of the double doors into a cold that made her think at first, Well, that's not so bad, but even before she'd walked the ten steps to the car, the cold began to slide its way under, pulling tight about her limbs. It didn't tingle like the cold she knew. It numbed her skin and slowed her movements. Sitting in the car she found herself thinking about itching her nose for a while before she actually did it.

They began to drive slow methodical circles about town,

passing down each back alley and driveway, scanning in the bright shifting light of the headlights every building and backyard. Light and dark slid across the snow in wild movements. Everything looked as if it were a polar bear motionless and staring, or leaping quickly away across the landscape.

The first time they reached the end of town near the dump, Maggie stopped the car. She looked around carefully and said, "This is where most of them sneak into town, once they've decided the dump doesn't have enough food for them." She put her hand on the door, picked up the rifle and said, "Stay here." She stepped out of the car.

Beryl felt the cold harsh against her face and then the door slammed and the car's heater hummed on. She hesitated before jumping out the other door. The snow squeaked beneath her feet and she was conscious of the dark behind her and the boulders off to her side. "What the hell are you doing?" she asked.

Maggie roared, "Get back in the car!"

Beryl felt the voice like wind on her ears. She got back in the car, sat with both hands open in front of her. She watched Maggie raise the binoculars and sweep them slowly across the rocks between the car and the dump. Maggie looked small against the darkness. Her hands held the binoculars by her face and she pointed her elbows out front as though waiting for a blow. The rifle hung over her shoulder. When she was done, she got back in the car.

Maggie put the rifle down and sat with both of her hands on the steering wheel. "Don't you ever," she said, "*ever* step out of this car. Not while it's night and I'm on a patrol. I don't care if a bear is playing jump rope with my intestines, you will not step outside. Is that clear?"

Beryl nodded. She sat very still.

"You're looking pale again." said Maggie. "Stop that." She looked away and then back. "God, you can look sickly." She started the car and backed out slowly onto the road. "I'm sorry. I should've warned you about that. The reason I get out of the car is 'cause I can spot them better. I've seen more bears there than anywhere else. Sometimes I can stop them from going into town. I shout or drive them away with the car. It's not like they're scared. More embarrassed. I think I've saved some bears that way.

"I stand out there and look, about three times an hour, thirty times each night, and I never feel calm about it. The rifle is mostly for my own comfort. It's a nice weight, you know, on my shoulder. I'm not allowed to shoot them unless it's clearly their life or mine. Sometimes I hope the sound of the gun will work as a distraction."

"Once, two years ago," Maggie said, "when I was out of the car, doing the circle, I turned too slowly. Something was glittering halfway up a hill. Couldn't make out what it was. When I continued my turn, I was suddenly looking through the binoculars at fur."

Maggie made a wavy gesture with her hand. Beryl didn't know if it was to show fur or to describe her emotions at the time.

"I pulled down my glasses. It was like I was trying to move

quickly, but everything got slower and slower. There was this bear, this huge bear, running at me, you know, swaying like they do, so goddamn big. Breathing, I could hear it. Black nose." Maggie put her fingers against her nose and held them there for a moment, thinking.

"Forty-five, fifty feet away, running forward. That nose for some reason was the thing I fixed on. Its black nose, all wet. I threw my binoculars as hard as I could at it, turned and got into the car. Still so damn slow. I had this thought, you know, this thought like someone else's voice in my head, that I wouldn't make it. I felt bad for my kids." She touched the car door on her side.

"I was pulling my left leg in when the bear hit the door, the window shattered in around me and the door slapped down on my calf, breaking it. I didn't feel the pain. I sort of heard a noise, but didn't feel anything. I looked out. This bear's face just filling my window. These furry jaws not four inches from my nose, not even a windowpane between us.

"It was so beautiful—the fur so clean. Very white. A young bear. It had bad breath, like a dog on a wet day. And then I was driving away, fast. The bear fell back to the ground. I don't even remember touching the gas."

Many times that night Beryl watched Maggie step out of the car, out into the dark silence of the Arctic. The snow squeaked loudly beneath her. Each time Maggie turned slowly in front of the car, scanning the rock piles ahead through the infrared binoculars, searching the night for white fur against white snow, or perhaps the bright reflection of eyes close enough to pick up the headlights. Each time Beryl scanned the snow also, watching for bears. She thought if anything happened, Maggie would have the gun. Beryl could do nothing but watch.

Beryl stared out the window into the dark. She imagined herself alone and warm, striding out across the snow, coming to a halt at the sound of the car, watching its bright lights whirl busily about in a tight circle, the two heads inside facing forward. She watched it depart, the sound of its engine muffled by the snow, her heavy white face turning to see its lights fade away around a corner.

"Why do you care about the bears?" Beryl asked.

Maggie said, "I don't really know. It's many things. To me they're beyond most animals 'cause they're unpredictable. They don't react the same way every time, like seals always diving, or muskox facing you, horns first. I've seen the same bear charge a car one day and run away the next. I even saw one roll over on its back and toss snow up in front of the headlights, wanting to play."

Maggie rubbed at her lower jaw with the inside of her thumb. "Once Jeff Shelbourne, a purely mean bastard, threw a steak out to a mother at the dump and while she was getting it, he shot both her cubs. In front of people too. Well, of course he was fined, but it's not like prison or anything." Maggie turned to look at Beryl, then back to the road. "Within a week that mother got Jeff while he was carrying the garbage out onto the porch. It was like she'd been waiting for him there on his porch, just sitting. I think she tracked him, I don't know. Jeff was the last polar bear fatality in this town. Three years ago."

Maggie worked the controls of the spotlight, its circle of visibility rolling silently across the snow. "I have great respect for the bears. They truly scare me."

Through the night Maggie and Beryl sang country ballads, camp songs, the themes from "The Brady Bunch" and "Speed Racer." Toward morning as the cold was even seeping into their mouths, Beryl told Maggie about how she wanted to go to all the wild places in the world photographing animals. "It's what David, the camera guy from the group, does for a living. But I want to do it differently. He likes the warm sunny places Club Med hasn't quite discovered. I want to go to the extremes: the Gobi Desert, Patagonia, Siberia. I've lived in a city all my life. The majority of my food comes wrapped in plastic. My home has central heating. My car has air-conditioning. Sometimes when I wake up in the morning I can't remember which season it is.

"I want to learn to survive on my own, to face extremes. I won't have really lived otherwise, not by the terms of this world, where there are rhythms like drought and cold, thirst and plenty. This may sound silly but sometimes I feel like my cat, still recognizable as a wild creature but neutered and declawed, made cuddly. She sits all day in the sun on the window ledge, watching life through the window."

Beryl realized they'd been talking for a while. In the long night, time passed differently. The sky was still black above but the drifts had begun to glow slightly in the dark. They'd seen nothing moving on the landscape all night long except the hissing dances of the snow.

Maggie nodded. "For me," she said, "I don't want travel. I want nothing but this place." She paused at an intersection, twisted about on the seat trying to see all around. She drove off to the right. "I'd like to stay up here, raise the kids. They won't live here when they're grown. I know that already. Still, I want my time with them. Sometimes when they say something new, I wonder where the hell they came from." Maggie touched her belly and added, "Not from here."

The car heater clicked on. Beryl felt a blast of heat across her face as dry as from an oven. Maggie said, "And I'd like to continue these patrols. To see the bears."

Beryl mentioned cautiously, "My dreams up here have been pretty weird." She glanced at Maggie, then looked at her hands held open on her knees. "A lot of them are about the bears, but not as if they're bears. They're dancing or we're having dinner. Isn't that weird?"

"No," said Maggie, looking out into the snow. "I dream like that all the time."

The two women looked at each other for a moment, and then away.

CHAPTER 12

After Beryl was followed by the bear, she often found herself sitting by the window of her hotel room, looking out. She felt differently now toward what she saw. She thought, I cannot go out there, not unless I'm in a car—even outside I have to stay in. The vast white prairie extended to the horizon beneath a solid blue sky. She still hadn't gotten used to the purity of the colors in this thin air, like scenes in a stained-glass window. Even the browns and grays of the houses in town were less muddy than down south, less dulled. She thought, All this and I can only look. As though it were already on David's film, playing on a flat screen.

She paced sometimes in her room. She thought she should be writing letters to people, making notes to herself, researching, but she couldn't think what to say about this place, or what to read. She certainly didn't want to go downstairs to the bar where David and Butler would be drinking, talking.

She would be seeing more than enough of them over the next month. She couldn't go outside, so instead she paced and looked out the window.

One afternoon, she noticed the wooden beams of the ceiling in her room, the thick hand-hewn wood of old colonial houses. She was surprised to find wood that beautiful in this town well beyond the tree line. She stood on a chair to touch one. It gave slightly beneath her fingers. They were made from Styrofoam.

"When I was a child," Maggie said, "I used to dream of being Alec Ramsey. He was this kid in these adventure books I read. He went to all these faraway countries with his black stallion and raced other horses, had adventures. Even though he was always told he couldn't do things at first because he was just a kid, he got to in the end because of his horse and because of his determination. I wanted to be just like him. I thought if I tried enough, I could be him. Only I was a skinny black girl who didn't have a big horse, didn't even have that many friends. I just read a lot. I dreamed of these adventures all the time, but in that heat down there I was too tired even to run across the yard."

The car fishtailed slightly in the deep snow and Maggie slowed down further to a crawl. "When I was twenty I found this man, this good man, who said he loved me. My mom thought he was all I would ever have. I married him immediately. I mean, it wasn't like I hadn't been trying to conform all the time. We had Julie and James. A lot of fighting. I couldn't believe in this role I was playing. I couldn't believe in the apartment and our marriage and the children. No, wait, it wasn't that I couldn't believe in the children. I believed in them more than anything, I just couldn't understand they were mine." Maggie's mouth twitched a little into a smile and she looked out at the snow.

"One day I saw an ad for people needed in the Arctic. They would pay for families to resettle. Gerry didn't have a job then. A month later we were here. He thought it was for a year. Thought this would finally keep me quiet. I thought so too until I stepped out of the plane and felt that wind across all that space. I'd never smelled anything like it, seen anything like it. Gerry left within the year. I really hope he's happier now."

Within a few years of college Beryl had already had a few photography shows and was making a steady living from freelancing for magazines. At her shows she'd begun to hear strangers say "Findham" a lot, as though by saying her name frequently during any discussion of her photos it would be obvious they understood her meaning. They would confidently ascribe to her name many qualities as though describing a substance like a rock with clear, easily definable veins. She still associated her last name with her parents and each time she heard it she saw her mother cocking the camera, her father adjusting the lights. In a way it was easier for her to imagine her parents taking the pictures all these people came to see.

When she was twenty-six she attended the show of a man three years older than she and as well-established. He specialized in photographing the insides of vegetables, magnifying to huge images the hidden seedy nooks and curls inside. She marveled at his technical expertise. One of his reviews, reprinted in foot-tall letters over the wine and cheese table, said his vision of the alien hidden future was focused, involuted and withering.

Beryl completely believed in his ability, his true claim to his reputation as an artist and a man with a vision. When they'd met she'd felt the firmness of his handshake, the width of his hand. Crow's-feet appeared around his eyes when he smiled; she assumed they came from peering into a camera and thinking hard. His teeth gleamed so white and smooth she'd known immediately that he didn't smoke or even drink coffee. He said he'd been to two of her shows. She noticed the way he concentrated directly on her face whenever she talked as though she were saying something quite complex and it was critical that he follow. When she turned away to get more wine, she'd also caught the way he glanced down her body. She felt honored and nervous, finished her glass of wine too quickly. She tried to smile the way she thought he thought she should: a small confident world-weary smile. They went out to dinner.

During the relationship she found herself copying his speech, his mannerisms. He tended to couch his own thoughts in what she considered the impersonal style of textbooks: "It can be assumed . . ." and "It need not be said . . ."

This style made what he said sound proven and factual. While talking philosophically he habitually brushed back his hair, massaging his scalp as though he were thinking so hard his head hurt. He twisted out his lips in grimaces while searching for the exact word. Her imitations of his speech never sounded as imposing. Her grimaces looked more like twitches than deep thought.

Gradually he took on the role of older teacher, gave her treatises by Krishnamurti, *The Moosewood Cookbook* and *Diet for a Small Planet*. He maintained that eating macrobiotic took less from the world. For her birthday he gave her a carton of recycled dioxin-free toilet paper and some perfume made without animal testing. She had been quite excited by the size of the wrapped package, then confused when she saw the first roll. He had explained the dangers of dioxins; once she saw he was serious she tried to thank him for the present as though delighted by the originality of his thought.

One day when he said she should do her laundry using only baking soda and vinegar, she'd listed all the chemicals he used in his photography. She meant only to tease him, but his face went quite stiff, the nostrils of his thin well-formed nose whitened.

"That," he said, "is Art. One cannot curtail the needs of one's expression, nor divert the means it chooses."

She had worked immediately at mollifying him. In the end he had relaxed only when she maintained that it was really the fault of scientists for not coming up with more ecologically sound chemicals. He was a passive victim from lack of choice. He had nodded his head at her wisdom and together they had decried the scientists' greed for profit.

And from the third breakfast they shared together, he had continually told her she should give up coffee.

"It is widely understood that there are three substances dangerous to clear vision," he said the first time he enumerated the evils of coffee. He held out his hand and counted off the items on his large, neatly manicured fingers. Those fingers last night had moved so cleverly across her body she'd almost been scared of them. Afterward she'd traced the outline and texture of his nails and wrists for a long time while he slept. The blond transparent hair on the backs of his knuckles had seemed so vulnerable, so delicate.

"Nicotine," he listed, "alcohol and coffee. Mystics around the world, from early Christians to modern-day Buddhists, agree that these three dull the spirit's sight." She watched his hands, looked at his red lips forming the words. "It's fairly obvious the connection between spiritual sight and art. We must have clear truthful vision."

She was fascinated by the idea that to photograph well, one's soul had to have clarity, as though it were another lens to be fitted onto the camera. Unfortunately she liked coffee. Each morning she made it quite strong using a melior, a ritual that helped her to wake up. He said that any awakening must come from within. Something about the weight with which he uttered advice like that made her see it as a country sampler stitched with little roses and hung on the wall. She knew this wasn't how he'd want her to hear his words.

When he was around in the morning she'd try to wait until he left to have her coffee, but sometimes he'd stay until lunch and then she'd pull the melior out in front of him. Once he asked how it felt to be addicted. Vocabulary about addictive behavior was quite popular at the time, from chemical dependency to dependent relationships. Several of her friends had confessed to her their addictions and she had felt insensitive and slightly left out that she had no confessions to give in return. She began to wonder if coffee would be acceptable.

"It's like seeing you drink ground glass," he explained. She smiled shyly at his caring, his protection, but each time she took a sip, he'd look away. She began to enjoy her coffee less and less.

For a week she experimented by not drinking caffeine to see if her photos actually did benefit. She couldn't see much of a difference. She wondered if it took longer than a week to work the impurities out of her soul.

He started to give advice about her work each time they met at her studio. He would state the criticism with his face turned a little away from the photograph so his eyes were narrowed and looking out from the side, the crow's-feet showing, the same pose he favored in the posters advertising his shows. She never ceased to revel in the physical size of his work, blown up to ten feet tall and fifteen feet wide, grainy and hard. Sometimes he nailed wood boards onto the pictures, dusted them with dirt, glued on telephone wiring that curved in and out. The vegetables looked quite alien, like the insides of machines. The critics loved his combination of photography and sculpture. She thought he couldn't have mistakes in pictures that big.

One day over lunch, he asked if she didn't sometimes tire of photographing only animals.

She had been raising a tofu curry sandwich to her lips. She put the sandwich back down. "What?" she asked.

"You only photograph animals," he said. "You must get tired of it. If you do that well with animals, you could say so many more things with a greater subject matter, with something more than . . ." He thought for a moment, puckered his lips out, and then laughed as he said, "Bambis and Thumpers."

She had tried to laugh at his joke. A drop of soyonnaise had clung to his upper lip. She'd leaned forward and wiped the drop away with her napkin, touching his lips with her other hand and then running her fingers down his chin, as though she could stop his voice, his words. She'd given up coffee almost entirely except sometimes in the afternoon if she still felt sleepy.

"Oh," she said, "I guess it would be nice if I had a larger scope, but animals are the only things that fascinate me enough to make the photos good."

"Maybe," he said, "you should try harder."

They had a long discussion on the subject. In arguments like this he was methodical and earnest, tracking each statement down to its logical conclusion. He would maintain that IF she had a limited subject matter, and IF she thought it would be better to photograph more things than animals, THEN she should try harder to increase her scope.

She wasn't as logical in her debates. For her the conversation wasn't the only thing going on. While they discussed the scope of her work, she noticed that when he made a point he held his hands cupped out toward her as though physically offering her something. She noticed that his eyes hardly ever rested on her, but tended to stare at the salt and pepper near her as though he were describing something as clear to him as the salt shaker's shape. She saw her own hands ripping up a napkin and wondered what she had in her fridge to make for dessert. After the argument he felt the issue had been settled and action would be taken. She felt they'd examined one side of it.

After he left she began to wonder. She heard his voice saying "Bambis and Thumpers" again and again.

The next time she saw him he handed her a portfolio showing his most successful work, so she could start to think about other subject matter. In the moment when her hand closed on the weight of the portfolio, she understood that he wouldn't let this issue drop. At some point she would enjoy photographing animals as little as she enjoyed drinking coffee now. The skin along her backbone began to sweat. Nothing in her life was worth more than her work.

After dinner, she kissed him one last time and then walked slowly home to change her phone number and leave on the first assignment she could find that lasted over a month.

Some of her best photos ever had come from that assignment photographing the new exhibits at the San Diego Zoo. She'd felt so lucky just being able to stand there for hour after hour watching the animals, holding her camera. Her patience had been inexhaustible. The pictures had an almost confidential feel to them, as though the animals were bending closer to show her something secret.

Once after that, at a company she worked for occasionally, she'd stepped around a corner in the hall to see him walking toward her, examining two photos in his hands. His hair had grown longer, his face thinner. She stepped back quickly around the corner and then into the women's room, breathing as unevenly as if she'd run for blocks.

She'd had other relationships since then, but they had been mostly physical with a clear line drawn by herself as to exactly how far the man could come into her life. Even with those who respected her rules, the relationships usually broke up within two or three months. She didn't know if it was just bad luck or if she imposed too many limits. Other women she saw, no matter how hurt they had been in the past, still tried with each new man to be as intimate as possible. She wondered if she was wrong not to do so.

Her last relationship had been the best, with a friend of a friend who had a pet otter she'd wanted to photograph. The man was as humorous and fast-moving as the otter, which had perfected the art of opening doors with its paws so it could join in on any water activity, from washing dishes to a shower. At the slightest slackening of her defense it would roll into the dishwater to curl up round a cup, ready to wrestle determinedly for ownership. Afterward, the dishes would have to be blown dry with a hair dryer to get rid of all the stray otter hair. When showering Beryl had learned not to jump at the otter's smooth fur slicking unexpectedly round her ankles.

The man and Beryl were both extremely ticklish and spent hours torturing each other, springing for the other's weak spots in unexpected moments and trying to defend their own, wriggling and laughing, begging for help. Once when they were going out to dinner, walking along a crowded city sidewalk all dressed up, he'd reached beneath her jacket as though to hug her waist closer to him and instead yanked her underwear halfway up her back. She yipped and twisted in pain and they fell to the sidewalk screaming insults and grabbing at each other's underwear. People passing them paused, looking back, faces blank and hostile.

After six months he brought up the possibility of moving in together. She told him she would think about it. That same week she drove the otter and him to a lake near the Maine border. At the lake the otter shot out of the car and down the mud bank on its smooth belly, tucking its head at the last moment into the water as if putting on a dress. It dove and frolicked, until it lay exhausted on its back in the water, its flat feline face tilted toward the sun. The man then stripped off his clothes and dove in, chasing the otter around the lake. At one point it scrambled up his back and onto his head, pushing him underwater with its weight so he surfaced sputtering. The otter swam back to nuzzle his coughing face, and the man grabbed its tail from behind to dunk it.

She watched them, feeling the sun on her back while she dabbled her toes in the cold black water. She sucked it all in with sharp bright happiness, the kind of happiness that made her skin prickle. She knew she would remember this day forever. She wondered if other people had a lot of these easy simple days. She thought if she moved in with him she'd be able to have this type of day all the time, and she felt a tight and vicious greed.

After that day at the lake, she felt more needy around him. She wanted that sort of happiness more often. She wanted nothing to threaten it. She watched for changes in him or in her feelings toward him. He said she should move into his place because it was bigger. When she went over to his house now she felt lucky each time she turned the front doorknob, a large wooden smiling sun. Each breakfast she ate there, she chose her spoon with care from his mismatched set of yard-sale silver. She felt pleasure holding each utensil, feeling its well-made balance and age-smoothed surface. She thought if she moved in there each detail would become normal instead, expected. The house would narrow with her knowledge and its repetition, and at the first fight it would become a cage. She knew sooner or later he would lose interest in her, he would tell her what to do. Every other man had done so. She began to fear this more and more, to withdraw from him. She said she wasn't so sure she wanted to move in at all.

Confused at first, he'd finally begun to argue with her.

Each time he yelled at her she felt joy, for she understood that this wasn't half so bad as she had imagined.

On the last day they fought with the kind of frenzied cruelty that can only pass between people who love each other. Fearful, the otter bit the base of her thumb badly. She still carried the scar, the clear imprint of sharp animal teeth across the meat of her palm.

CHAPTER 13

Each day it got colder. At the town dump, Beryl began to have problems with her cameras. They stuck and the battery needed to be warmed against her belly before it would work. She felt stupid that she hadn't anticipated the extent of this problem. Back in Boston she'd thought if she just kept a spare camera warming inside her parka at all times, she could switch them as needed. However, when she developed some of the film in the town newspaper's darkroom, she found the pictures had fine lines etched across them as though she'd shot them through the glass of a broken lens.

When she showed David, he said, "Oh, that's the emulsion freezing and then cracking. What a ridiculous climate. Why on earth do people live up here while Florida still has lots available? Keep the cameras warm and be real careful rewinding the film. Do it slowly, by hand. In this sort of cold, static electricity builds up. If you rewind quickly, the static'll discharge and you'll get a pretty lightning fork across your best images."

In spite of their care David and Beryl's problems increased. They stacked spare cameras near the car heater, but the buttons still stuck, the batteries slowed. David would push at the controls again and again, swearing.

Butler phoned the magazine's headquarters in New York for some heaters for their cameras, but he said they couldn't expect anything for at least a week. David began to keep his camera plugged into the car's battery for extra electricity, the long cord snaking across the van and sometimes winding around David's feet six or seven times while he followed the circuitous movements of a bear. Beryl continued to keep two extra cameras always inside her parka, a single layer away from her skin, switching cameras every five minutes. Even with long underwear between her stomach and the cold metal, she would feel the slow chill, the numbness sneaking across her hips and up her back.

In this cold, her hands also began to slow up. She could feel the lethargy in her fingers as she tried to focus, then shoot. She fought the frustration. She wanted that picture, that one now. Her fingers moved too late. The gloves fumbled. The camera hummed sickly, trying to wind itself forward. After twenty minutes with her upper body out of the van, she could feel the cold invading her movements. When David touched her shoulder, her descent took long seconds, her knees complaining.

One day when she was rewinding some film it actually

snapped clear through the center, the knob spinning free. When she opened the camera in the darkroom the broken ends of the film were shattered as finely as glass. There'd been a picture on that roll of a bear lying on its back, arms limp across its flat chest, looking toward her with its dark eyes. The bear had looked sleepy, patient and very human. It didn't have the flat gaze of a bird or fish; it had regarded her with an expression, a presence.

In this cold she felt much older, an aging woman whose body didn't work properly. She understood why Jean-Claude walked so slowly, why he didn't smile. Once you had known the power of such cold for extended periods, every movement would seem an effort.

She knew her slowness might also be caused by lack of sleep. Each night that week she'd snuck out with Maggie for the first three hours of her watch, then Maggie would drop her back at the hotel. Each night Beryl climbed slowly up the stairs to her room, fumbled with the keys, her fingers wooden. She had to work even to pull her gloves off. She would run cold water across her hands and face, feel the water burn, the prickling. She turned the temperature of the water up slowly and the skin of her face itched as it warmed. She rubbed cream into her skin, then crawled into her bed, the clean rustling of the sheets surprising her, any sounds surprising her other than the car's hum and the slow beat of the windshield wipers against the snow. Beryl closed her eyes, seeing only the snowy dark houses rolling past the windows.

She'd yet to see a bear when she was with Maggie on the night patrols, very unusual for this time of year. Maggie said she was seeing five to seven of them after Beryl left in the hours before dawn. Maggie and Beryl continued to drive slowly about the town, scanning, watching. Beryl needed to see a bear striding calmly through the town, owning it, far from the dump and the mayonnaise jars. She wanted to see a bear in the depths of the night, judging the height of a window, the people inside sleeping.

As Beryl developed her early pictures, she found that she hadn't captured the arctic light at all. Those pictures un-damaged by the cold looked almost like cleverly disguised zoo shots. She wanted the crystal bright light, the wide-open space, the bear's swaying amble forward. She tried slower, then faster film, different filters, wide-angle lenses. After a while she got the sense of space, the size of the bear, but still she hadn't captured that light within her camera, trapped it on her film. She wanted to bring that light back with her.

Friday morning Butler told the group about a man who had been stalked and killed the previous year while driving a bulldozer along the Trans-Alaska Pipeline.

"Bears," Butler said, then paused to take a sip of his coffee. He sucked the hot liquid in through his teeth with his lips grimacing wide. Beryl guessed he had picked up that habit while drinking coffee from thin metal cups on camping trips. He probably thought it made him look tougher. "Bears have no fear of large machinery. They are used to ice shifting beneath them, to cracking sounds and loud movement. The bulldozer operator couldn't hear anything over the motor. He was strapped into the seat. I mean, even if he'd heard the bear's steps behind him, what could he have done? A bulldozer won't move faster than five miles an hour. There was nowhere to hide or run. Just flat snow, rocks, gravel in all directions. Just the road he drove on leading back to base. Everything flat." Butler pushed his plate away and stretched his arms out across the back of the booth. His shoulder cracked.

Beryl was sitting beside him and she glanced up at his arm lying just above her shoulders. She had to lean forward a bit to avoid resting her head against the inside of his elbow.

Butler continued. "They think the bear started eating the guy while he was still on the moving machine." Butler looked down at Beryl beside him, searching her face for disgust. She found it difficult to look tough returning his stare when she was crouched slightly forward.

"The road," said Butler, "lay so straight, the bulldozer ran on for another mile before it got stuck in a wall of snow it had built earlier. They think the bear took the man's body away a little before that. They found what was left of the body about a mile away."

Beryl considered this type of death. It might be sudden and you wouldn't know what had happened, but just as likely it would be slow. The bear wouldn't care if you were dead or alive just so long as you were immobilized. You'd be thinking your normal thoughts on a normal day, your hearing dulled by the loud machine you sat astride, only your vision remaining. You'd see an empty flat landscape, scarred straight down the center by the road. You'd fidget in your seat in hopes of speeding this day along, of getting to the end of it to your TV and some dinner.

Abruptly a force grabs you, so powerful you don't even feel the pain. Just a wind, a crack at the back of your head. You're twisted about, blinking, looking up at a creature whose size and violence you'd never have believed, whose eyes are black and wet and small and when it leans forward to bite the flesh of your belly, you feel the rough thick hairs of its neck against your face.

"The man's body was completely mauled," Butler added, leaning in a little closer to Beryl. He did not look at Jean-Claude or David while he told the story. He was watching for her reactions. She saw his nostrils flare a little as he breathed in the smell of her skin. "Beryl, tell me if this is too gory for you, but he had no right leg." Butler watched Beryl for weakness, some trace of disgust or terror.

"He had no right leg and—you know how bears like body fat—he did not have much skin left." Butler paused to gauge her reaction to this information.

She tired to keep her face slack. His eyes narrowed slightly in irritation. She'd begun to feel uneasy around him. She didn't think she would feel this way if they spent less time around each other, but she spent most of the day within ten feet of him. If she'd met him in Boston she might've enjoyed his company for the stories he told. She might have felt attracted to him. Instead she knew she was going to be spending the next month with him in a small bus. His body weighed almost twice as much as hers. The fabric of his shirt stretched and wrinkled with the slow movements of his breath. He stood closer to her than she liked people to stand.

Butler continued. "They don't know how long he lived after the bear attacked him. But the doctors said that no one of his wounds was fatal. He could have lived through all of it, died slowly after the bear left, of cold and loss of blood, lying on the snow." Butler held out his heavy hand warped into claws, moved the thick paw forward slowly to touch her face, to run the nails along her cheek. He wanted to scare her, to force her to show fear. The rest of the team watched her reaction.

She moved back from his reach, not out of fear of the bear, but out of revulsion at Butler's warm moist flesh. He smiled.

She thought that being mauled by a bear was a better way to die than most. It was better than listening to the uneven rasp of your respirator.

CHAPTER 14

Saturday morning, someone knocked on the door of her room. When she opened the door she was surprised to see Jean-Claude. He held out a bag of wiring and batteries. "I think I can make a heater for your camera," he said. Standing face to face with him, she realized he was only two or three inches taller. She wondered if he'd been fed properly when he was a child; perhaps the expeditions he'd been on at fourteen had stunted his growth. Or maybe he had simply needed to be short, to eat less, to move fast in order to survive. His white eyebrows gave his serious face an almost comical look of shock.

He helped her rig a small battery-operated heater on the bottom of her camera. He worked methodically, explaining the steps. He spoke clearly, succinctly. He checked each connection three times. She wondered what his parents were like, his childhood. She wanted him to talk about his trips, about the Arctic, the cold and death, what he thought of walking across the snow away from a pile of clothes filled with something once alive. She watched his movements carefully. His hands were large and calloused. His right hand seemed bigger than his left. After a few minutes of staring she realized that his left hand had only three fingers; even the knuckle of the fourth finger had been removed. His fingers moved precisely, gracefully. She wondered if his mind was also moving the finger that was no longer there.

Next, as Jean-Claude watched, she constructed a heater for David. She watched her own hands and tried to move them as precisely as Jean-Claude had moved his. She imagined that her whole life depended on the success of this machine. No backup wiring or batteries. No shelter or extra food. Not even time. She rechecked the links again. Turned it on. The warmth rose, slow and comforting.

She smiled up at Jean-Claude and realized she only played with a terror he had lived.

"Hey," Beryl asked, "can you also look at my parka and clothes for the cage? I got everything the magazine recommended but I'm still worried about sitting outside in the wind. Do you mind?" In Maggie's car, even with all her gear on and the heater going full blast, Beryl's feet and fingers went numb, while her back sweated against the seat.

She opened the closet, pulled out everything and laid it across the bed. She'd brought two suits of polypropylene underwear, three flannel shirts, several Icelandic sweaters,

Thinsulate pants, Gore-Tex overpants, the green and gleaming parka that zipped up to a small hole for breathing and vision, two pairs of gloves, three hats, six battery-powered wool socks, boots large enough for moon landings, goggles and a face mask. Each piece of clothing was emblazoned with the insignia of the *Natural Photography* company. She disliked wearing the electric socks the most, for they always smelled lightly of burning wool. She hadn't turned them on after the first day; the smell made her too nervous. She imagined her feet catching fire. The clothing took up an impressive amount of space, much more of the bed than she did when she lay down.

Beside her, Jean-Claude started shaking. At first she thought he trembled from some sort of flashback to an expedition, to the cold and the want. She thought briefly about backing slowly out of the room. Then she looked at his face and saw that he was laughing. He held the back of his hand against his mouth and his face had changed so completely he almost looked like the boy of twenty he was.

She looked back at the pile of clothing and began to smile. When she walked to Maggie's car with all of the clothing on, she breathed as slowly and stiffly as an astronaut.

"I'm sorry," he said, turning to her. His face grinned young and happy. At that moment she could almost imagine him holding books under his arm and talking about grades. He said, "You could drown in all that. The Inuit clothing is better. Warmer. Come to my room. I have an extra suit."

Jean-Claude's suit had two separate layers. On the inside was a shirt and pair of pants of caribou skin. The outside was made of wolf hide, with wolverine trim about the face.

"Put the caribou layer against the skin," Jean-Claude explained. "No clothing underneath. Fur faces out." He ran his fingers over the nap of the caribou. "Wear the outside layer with the fur facing in. Don't need anything else but socks, boots and gloves. With the body warm, the face can take intense cold. Has to. Masks simply freeze with the moisture from breathing.

"Ice is a problem. Out there." Jean-Claude's eyes shifted to look out the window. Beryl watched them move slowly back to her. "You sweat and exhale moisture. It freezes to your clothing. This suit is made of fur, doesn't retain ice. If you fall in water or sweat really hard, take it off and shake it. The ice shatters off. It's dry again. Not like wool, where the moisture invades the cloth."

She went into the bathroom to try the suit on. His shelves were bare except for a toothbrush and toothpaste. She coughed to cover the noise of opening the medicine cabinet. Only a hairbrush. Beneath the sink was a first-aid kit big enough to be a doctor's bag.

She stripped and pulled the suit on. The caribou skin ran down over her chest and arms, supple, soft and light. She pulled on the pants and tied the thongs at the waist. She smelled smoke and leather, the sweat of sled dogs and Jean-Claude, a working smell like bitter wood. The short thick fur of the caribou stood out from her body. She could feel the stitches on the inside along her belly and shoulders, but they were so small and tight she couldn't see them even when she brushed back the hair. She pulled the outer layer on. The thick fur rustled over her face. As the hood settled into place, she breathed in a musk as thick and sweet as skunk: wolverine or wolf. The smell dissipated almost immediately. She didn't know if she'd gotten used to it already or if it faded quickly in the fresh air.

She stood in the white tiled bathroom, light and flexible. With each movement she made, the fur of the two layers shivered and brushed up against each other. The fur made no sound; rather, it created a distinct feeling like when the hair on her neck stood up, that feeling all across her body, the interlocking and giving of bristles. It seemed she had always waited for this feeling, the soft skin of a caribou brushing up between her legs. She felt strong and big. She looked at herself in the full-length mirror. She was surprised at her new mass, the smells she encompassed. She wondered if this was how the bears felt.

She went into the bedroom to show Jean-Claude how the suit fit. He pulled the hood forward over her head as far as it would go. She could feel the wolf fur against her cheeks. He pulled at the bottom of the parka to make sure it went down far enough, then swept the front of it up and back to look at the way she'd knotted the thongs of the pants.

"No," he said, "never double-knot these." Her stomach was exposed. His hand held the material of the parka up against her ribs. If he pulled on the thongs to see how tight they were, he would see her pubic hair. "You have to untie the pants to shit and pee. If you take off your gloves for the knot, you could lose your fingers." He let go of the material, stepped back a bit. "It's like the moon out there. Have to think ahead." He tapped the side of her head. "Think all the time. Can't touch metal. Must protect your eyes. How deep is the snow? Your lips frozen? Hands still work? Should you run to warm up now or will you need that energy later?"

The smells and Beryl's own heat came up to her through the neck of the suit. The sensations melded together into the feeling of a single body. Always before when she had stood, clothed or unclothed, in front of a man's gaze she had felt deficient, too small. Now she stood in the smells and skins of many bodies and felt herself to be larger than she'd ever been.

He told her that if she'd worn the clothing *Natural Photography* recommended into the cage, she wouldn't have been able to move enough in its bulky mass to clap her hands to stay warm. Every year they sent people up here like that, and it was fine so long as they stayed inside heated cars or houses. But when they tried to go out on the snow for a while, things happened.

When Jean-Claude stood up from checking the length of the suit's legs, she found herself blushing. He said he was concerned that the suit might be too tight. He pushed back the hood, reached into the back of the neck to make sure there was enough room for the extra heat to escape. His arm stretched up and over her shoulder, his body leaning forward against the outer fur. She felt the smooth imprint of each of his three fingers against the bare skin between her shoulder blades. The wolf skin rustled.

Back in the bathroom she pulled the suit off and put her own clothes on with regret. Her clothing seemed scentless, plain and light without the fur. Zippers were inordinately mechanical, buttons foreign. Holding the suit in her arms, she returned to the other room. There was a chair in the corner, but she sat down beside Jean-Claude on the bed. He looked at her, then away. His eyes roved slowly over the blank white walls. She wondered what he looked for. She shifted slightly closer to him on the bed. She wanted to touch his skin, to find out if it was warmer than average. Perhaps he was a small furnace like Maggie.

Jean-Claude said, "When the British explored the Arctic, they wore the normal navy uniform. Weren't allowed anything else. They thought nothing could be as good as two layers of British woolens."

Beryl was glad he was finally talking. She wanted him to continue. "Didn't they cheat?" she asked. "Once they got here, didn't they ignore the rule?"

"Difficult to smuggle other clothes on board. Certainly couldn't wear them in public. The officers punished that." Jean-Claude looked at the wall as though he read the words there. She wondered if he cared who he was talking with. She wondered if he had any friends, any siblings. "Each year a boat was trapped in the ice. The ice floes would grind together over the months. The boat's hull would crack. The men froze or starved slowly. Winter's nine months long here. Most of it's a single night. With no sun, they could be awake at noon or three in the morning. It didn't matter, still dark. They could stay awake for two hours or twenty. Didn't matter. Time passes slowly that way."

Beryl watched his hands. They lay in his lap, too big and heavy for the rest of his body. They had thickened knuckles and deep calluses. She wondered if they hurt.

He turned to look at her for a moment. "In situations like that," he said, his words clear and careful, "you've got to understand what you live for, exactly. You've got to be able to hold on to it. If you don't have it, or if you forget, you die."

He watched her. She wasn't sure how to respond to what he'd said. It seemed he was waiting for something. "It must be a horrible death," she offered.

He turned away. She couldn't tell if he was satisfied or not. "There was this one Dutch captain. The ship ran into an iceberg. It's easy to do. Some of the floes are the size of city blocks, switching directions with the wind. The captain ran forward, his hands held out like this." Jean-Claude put his hands up in front of him, his shoulders pushing behind. "Ran up to the floe, placed his hands against the ice. He was sucked down between the ship and floe. His men watched it. He'd been a good captain." Jean-Claude let his hands fall back into his lap.

"Part of his ship survived. It fell over on the ice with seven men inside. They had no food. They had no wood but the piece of the ship around them. They slowly burnt it in pieces.

They floated about on the ice. They bled one another in turn, drank the blood from a shoe. After a month a man went out onto the ice to kill himself. He saw another ship passing. They were rescued."

Jean-Claude turned toward her. His face was blank. He held his hands palm up in a gesture she didn't understand.

She reached out and ran her fingertips across his palm. The skin was thick and hard, split open in places. Warm. She pulled her hand back and smiled at him, embarrassed.

Jean-Claude looked at her, confused, suddenly very young.

CHAPTER 15

On their last night in town they all stayed around after dinner talking until late. They drank and looked hungrily about at strangers passing by the table. None of the four attempted to talk to any other people. So far as Beryl knew, only she and Jean-Claude actually knew anyone in town. Jean-Claude seemed to know every person who walked by smelling of dogs and gasoline. Each one looked around at the *Natural Photography* group and then gave Jean-Claude a silent nod. He nodded back.

Most of the people he knew were men, but Beryl noticed one woman. Small with dark eyes. Beryl looked to see how Jean-Claude nodded back. She could tell nothing from him, his patient steady gaze, his precise nod. She realized she was getting quite curious about his life.

David began to talk about his home in southern California. He said, "I live right on the beach with a friend, near San

Diego. We got the place in order to snorkel there. We used to snorkel every day. I like the silence, you know, the light and the fish. So much movement and color in such a small area." David breathed out through his mouth. "I never filmed that world there. I never wanted to, you know?" He looked about at them.

"In the last few years, though, it's changed. I don't know what happened. It wasn't anything abrupt, not any one thing, just all the developments, all the new towns, a small oil spill." He picked up his napkin and rubbed his thumb across its edge. "Now when I walk down to the beach, the sound is the same. The sun is the same, the waves. But I wade into the surf and the water is empty." He put the napkin down.

Beryl watched Butler as David talked. He seemed slightly confused by the story, or perhaps by other clues, by the way David mentioned his "friend." Butler looked at David's face and then, for some reason, at his hands. He shifted his chair away from David, but not far. He still looked confused.

David pestered Jean-Claude to do some calls of arctic animals. Jean-Claude finally agreed.

"Snow grouse," he said, pulling his upper lip in and making the clucking and whispering calls of the white bird with the astonished eyes, the bird that slept beneath the drifts each night and in the morning stuck its head up through the snow like a periscope. Space and cold echoed in his calls as physical as a touch on Beryl's face.

Jean-Claude didn't move his hands to make the call. He

simply fixed his eyes on open space, pursed his mouth and made the noise. Beryl assumed he didn't use his hands because when he needed to do these calls outside, his hands would be covered by gloves.

"Arctic fox," he said next. He barked and yipped the small voice of the scavenger, busy, hungry, constantly complaining.

"The wolf." He craned his neck upward and Beryl watched the sound roll up from the bones of his chest. A howling, curling call that poured out and quieted the entire dining room at the first note. The sound of speed and power, of loneliness and snow. A roomful of faces turned to look at him.

Jean-Claude put his head down. He blinked at all of them, then around at the dining room. He didn't seem to realize that his imitation would attract any attention. Someone dropped a fork clattering to the floor. With the silence broken, people shifted a little in their seats. The dining room quickly returned to normal.

Beryl asked about the polar bear, what sounds it made.

Jean-Claude turned to her, looking for a second without recognition. Then he spoke. "The polar bear makes no noise. It's a loner. No need to talk to other bears, except in raising cubs or when angry. The only sounds are from its breath."

She thought of its noises—hissing, chuffing, the snow settling back after its black-bottomed paws have already moved on.

Beryl was the first one to say good night. She had to get dressed in order to meet Maggie for the night's patrol. She walked up the stairs to her room, feeling warm and fairly drunk. Looking down the staircase at the three men laughing and talking together, she set about carefully memorizing the scene. She knew this would be as good as it got.

After she got dressed in the *Natural Photography* suit, she went around the back hall to the parking lot where Maggie was to meet her. She had decided in the end not to wear Jean-Claude's suit because she thought Maggie would tease her. Also, she found the long night in the car quite cold; although she liked the feel of the fur suit, she thought she would rather experiment with it during the relatively short periods she would spend in the cage.

She stepped outside into the unheated tunnel that led to the parking lot. The warm air from the hotel steamed and swirled around her, then disappeared. Her face numbed so quickly that her eyes blinked a few times in shock. The air was colder than she'd ever felt. She walked down the concrete tunnel listening to the echo of her breath and the squeak of the snow. Her limbs felt loose and her thoughts a bit slow. Being a little drunk probably helped in this kind of cold. Dimly, beyond the walkway, she heard the hum of what seemed to be a large motor. She thought it might be Maggie waiting for her in the car and sped up.

She turned the handle and pushed open the final set of doors. They jerked wide, pulling her with them. Her parka snapped hard in the wind. She skidded sideways, arms out. Snow filled her eyes and nose. Instinctively she twisted her back to it, crouched down. Then the wind roared from another direction and she twisted back around and stood cautiously up, one glove shielding her face.

She could not see the hotel.

She turned again. Snow covered her eyelashes. She could hear nothing but the uneven snap and scream of the wind. The air and ground whirled white, curving into each other, no farther away than an outstretched arm. The wind roared up her legs, ballooned out her parka, rolled across her belly. Her skin deadened instantly at its touch. It ached deeper down, throbbing.

She wasn't sure at all where the hotel should be.

Looking down she could see nothing below her knees. The snow hissed and flowed about her like a river. The wind jerked at her ankles. She tried to curl her toes in, then out. She couldn't tell if they moved at all. She was sobering quickly. She knew she couldn't stay still.

She began to walk across the snow toward where she thought the hotel might be, taking small steps so she wouldn't fall with the sudden shoves of the wind. Her face hardened with cold. She was sure that sooner or later she would hit the hotel or one of the houses on the street.

She held one arm out in front of her. The snow immediately covered it, whitened it. The snow whirled thicker around her until she could barely see the glove on the end of her arm. The wind hit her hard in the side, the back, then the arm. She swayed and moved each foot forward in its baby step, her arm waving. She could see small drifts building up on the wrinkles of the parka. She breathed slower and slower.

She could no longer feel her feet hit the ground. She couldn't even see her feet. She shifted each leg on through the tide, floating.

She thought she must have walked a hundred feet through the snow, certainly at least fifty. The street couldn't be wider than that. She still hadn't hit a building. She wondered if she could be walking in circles. Without being able to see any landmark, with the battering wind, it was hard to hold a straight line. It seemed as though she was going directly forward. She wondered if she could be walking between the buildings, by people's back steps and driveways, or straight down the street toward the end of town into the open tundra beyond. She tried edging off to the left.

After a while she could no longer feel the arm held out in front of her. She edged off to the right. From above, her path must seem quite confused, staggering around, arm waving. An adult playing pin the tail on the donkey, late at night, all alone. She walked on slowly like Jean-Claude, knowing his cautious balanced limp.

Abruptly she decided she must be outside of town by now; that was why she wasn't hitting any buildings. She turned around the way she'd come, but going back directly along her path wouldn't work. She knew the hotel wasn't that way. Perhaps a bit to the left. She stood there, leaning into the wind, confused.

The wind slapped her hard on the right. Her feet slid out from under her. She didn't feel herself hit the ground. She struggled up. Her legs slid in the snow. Her arms wouldn't lift. How silly, she marveled. And how quick. The wind knocked her back down. She felt very small in the face of all this power, a child, a baby. The snow cushioned her face, soft as a blanket. Her heart beat slow and full against the cold of her limbs. She listened to it. The center of her body felt warm.

The snow swirled across her face and up her nose. She coughed.

She thought, Lazy, and got to her hands and knees. She had a hard time knowing what they did. Her wrists wouldn't move the way she wanted, her feet dragged behind her. This all seemed like such a simple mistake to her, warmth such an easy luxury. Her left sleeve had pulled up a bit. She could see the skin of the wrist. Blue-white.

She looked at it and was surprised to realize that she was dying.

She crawled forward, rocking. She concentrated on keeping her balance. Her body drifted away from her bit by bit. She could feel nothing now but the air sucking down into her lungs. She could see nothing but the edges of her hood and her wrists sliding forward through the soup. The blood pushed in her ears, her limbs limped across the snow. The sounds filled her head, such strong noises, each thump and sigh, each rustle and drag.

She remembered the sounds of brushing her hair last night before she slept, the whisk and pull of the brush across her scalp. She remembered stepping into her bath the night before she left Boston, her toes flushing suddenly pink in the hot water. She saw the polar bear burning crisply, running over the hill, the sounds of her breath and the crackle of the fire. She moved on four legs like the bear.

She thought, Live, and crawled on. She imagined her parents sitting in their living room in Boston, the television on, the blue light across their faces, their hands lying loose and open two inches from each other.

Ahead she saw something solid within the shifting of her world. She saw more than one object ahead. If she could only cover her face, she thought, she would be warm. If she could only close her eyes.

The first object was a bear. The butt and side of a giant bear, a white bear defined in negative against the blue of the open car door and Maggie's parka lying below. Maggie's black hair poured out of the hood, wet with blood. Maggie's arm waved in the air. Beryl was close, crawling closer.

The bear turned to face Beryl, dropping the front of Maggie's parka from his mouth. He was a giant, yellow with age, a low mean head moving toward her. His fur ruffled with the wind and the snow he was made of. His eyes narrowed, his teeth white against the black gums of his mouth. She crawled toward him.

The bear pushed up and stood to such a height she lost his face in the snow above. She could smell his warm thick stink of meat and piss and damp fur. He swiped his arms about. She crawled forward toward the heat. She crawled forward into the bow of his body, the bow of his legs. Her head bumped against his testicles, her nose wiggled itself deep within the private heat of his fur until it touched the skin beneath, dry and smooth like talcum powder. She touched her nose to this and breathed deeply of this sanctuary. Her face would warm.

She felt the bear stiffen. She felt the fur fly up. She saw the bear above her leaping up into the snow. She was alone.

She heard a small noise. A kind of chortle, a kind of snort. She looked all around and then down and there Maggie laughed as hard as she could with her cheek gaping open, ripped to the bone to show the teeth and gums. Beryl could see the mechanics of laughter in all their glory.

Maggie sat up and hugged her. Beryl stilled for a moment within the gesture, then placed her head deep within the hug, within the arms, burrowing deep into the warmth. Beryl made a noise like a cough, mouth distorted and unwilling. Maggie began to cry. The tears froze against the skin of her cheeks. The two of them crawled slowly up and into the car. They closed the door and sat.

The wind blew outside. There was a silence, a stillness, as deep as any Beryl had ever imagined. It poured slowly across her skin until Maggie threw the whole of her leadened weight down onto the horn and the snow by the front bumper pushed back into hotel doors and people were helping them in.

CHAPTER 16

The hospital released Maggie before Beryl. Maggie's injuries to face, shoulder and hip needed only stitches. She had no frostbite, for she hadn't been outside long enough. There would be scars though, the doctor warned her. Maggie said she was glad; the town would feel too guilty to ever take her job away from her now. Also, she said, scars would scare the kids, make them mind her more.

The doctor worried more about Beryl. The skin flaked and peeled off her arms, legs and back as though she'd lain too long in the sun. At first she felt pain like hot water being poured across her skin, then the slow irresistible itching. She scratched luxuriously everywhere, even leaning up against the headboard of the bed and wriggling her back like a deer against a tree. She smoothed on the lotion the doctor gave her. The fresh pink skin beneath made her look like a newborn baby emerging from the shell of her old body. And as though her body were new, she felt a great awe of it, for pulling her through the storm. She held each limb carefully, measuring its width with her hand, tracing the bones beneath the cover of flesh, studying her body with clear admiring eyes. Her gentlest touch hurt the places that had been frostbitten. Her wrists turned an angry red for a while after the dead skin flaked off, and she slept holding both wrists off the sides of the bed like a hawk soaring.

On the second day the doctor told her the smallest toes had been removed from both her feet.

Beryl looked down at her bandaged toes. She couldn't tell. At first she thought maybe he was just kidding, hoping to scare her. They would have taken her toes while she was unconscious that first night. She didn't know what they did with them afterward. She imagined herself wandering around the hospital, rummaging through garbage cans. She imagined herself finding the toes, small and white and fat, smooth slivers of the nails, curled tightly together as babies.

The doctor had wide cheekbones, black hair. Beryl wondered if he were part-Inuit, but he could also have been Hawaiian. He said he was amazed that Beryl had survived as well as she had. He advised her to show some caution in this world that had almost killed her.

Beryl nodded. The hospital seemed airy and far away. Sometimes she had a problem paying attention to people's words. She looked down instead at her tingling body, awed.

No one could convince her to give up the expedition.

Butler visited her on the first day and explained, "*Natural Photography*'s asked me to send their regrets about this whole incident. They say if you're willing to sign a paper saying you won't sue, they'll understand if, with the shock of this whole thing, you want to get out of your contract." He pursed his lips in thought, and she noticed again their thick beauty. "Don't worry about the project. I've seen this happen before. It'll still be done in time. They'll just scramble for a few days to find someone. Someone'll fit in the cage."

While Butler talked, he kept looking at her white-wrapped toes. He looked away from her face. He seemed uncomfortable and sad. He picked at his fingers, pulling at the cuticles. She realized he probably gave money to charities that showed children and mothers suffering. He looked smaller sitting in the bare white hospital room. She guessed that for himself he hoped for a good clean death, something violent, a falling tree or charging moose, while he was still in his prime. He wouldn't want to watch the slow decrease of his body, because he knew clearly that he was stronger than most humans, faster, taller. He felt proud of that. She knew she was smaller, weaker, slower than the average. She felt pride that her body existed at all, that it struggled on. From now on she would fight relentlessly for every breath.

"But Butler," she said, "I've no intention of suing *Natural Photography* and there's nothing that could dissuade me from finishing the expedition."

He looked her straight in the eye. She could see he hadn't expected her to want to finish.

"I'm glad," he smiled. "Real glad." He left soon, saying she needed her rest.

David asked her if she'd gotten any of it on film. He looked hurt that she hadn't asked him to join the patrols. During the four days they waited for her to heal, he went out each night with Maggie, filming.

"I got some great shots," he told her, shifting in his seat in excitement. "You know, white bears trotting forward through darkness, long black shadows behind. I got 'em with this megaspotlight I borrowed from Maggie. She's neat. Real fun to talk to. The spotlight's intense. The bears look wicked, every hair on their bodies glowing with power.

"The narration," he said, "will be a cinch. You know the kind: a deep male voice, probably British, reciting facts. Long pauses, the bear's breathing piped over." David panted deep and raspy a few times.

He paused then and looked down the hospital bed to her feet. He shook his head, and when he spoke his voice was slower, quieter. "You know, you don't have to worry about the cage if you don't want to. You wouldn't inconvenience anyone. No one would think less of you. Really. I could do it. No problem. I know how to handle a still camera."

When she told him that she still wanted to finish the expedition, he laughed.

"Stubborn fool," he said. "But it's a good thing, 'cause I don't know dick about a still camera. And, you know, I would've thought less of you."

He leaned forward, touched her arm where the skin tingled when she rubbed cream into it, tingled as though she were still just warming up. Less skin flecked off each time, the flesh beneath blushing red. David held her arm. He asked, "You're not scared of the bears now, are you?"

The first day Jean-Claude visited, he said, "You should stay here as long as you want. You aren't holding us up. The bus still hasn't arrived." The bus was their transportation for the next leg of the trip.

"When's it due?" asked Beryl.

"Monday morning." The company had missed the deadline twice now. Jean-Claude turned his head away then toward the window and made his only nervous gesture; he ran the balls of his fingers back and forth over the wood arms of his chair.

Jean-Claude visited for long periods, sitting beside her. Most days he did not even say as much as he had about the bus and if she hadn't been so tired and drugged up, she might have felt nervous, responsible for a conversation. Only later did she realize that if she'd tried to talk more he probably would have left. As it was, he seemed to feel more and more at ease.

At first Jean-Claude lay his hands across his legs as he usually did, stretched out and empty, but once when she woke up he was holding her hand, cupping it within his own. He didn't look at her as she slowly sat up. She wondered if he'd picked up her hand because that was what one was supposed to do when visiting sick people, or if he was trying to heat the frostbite out. The warmth of his hands comforted her, harsh as a heated rock held to the face. Round her bandages and raw skin, she could feel the deep cracks in his hands from the cold and the dryness. She liked the touch of his human palms. Sometimes she remembered the bear's powdery flesh against her nose. She'd made no comment to Jean-Claude. They continued their silence.

From then on when he visited he conscientiously held each hand in turn. She kept her hands still, relaxing them into his hardened palms. She sensed that acceptance from him was rare. Her hands healed more each day. His care reminded her of when she was a child and her mother had held the wet cool washcloth against her fevered forehead, the hand cupped firm and worried over her brow and cheek.

While he visited they both faced the window, watching the frost grow slowly across the glass. She slept a lot those days with him nearby; she had fewer nightmares with him around. She'd begun to dream each night that she crawled through the storm in her hospital clothes and the bear paced just ahead of her, slowly unzipping his head with his curved yellow nails.

For days after the blizzard she felt sleepy and ate more than normal, as though she'd been drained over a period of weeks.

One night when she woke panting, silently struggling under the covers to crawl forward, to survive, he placed both his hard hands against her face, pulled her up close against him. "Beryl," he said, "you're safe. You're warm. Wake up." His shoulder smelled like grass.

When she began to gasp and then to cry, he held her still for a while and said, "It's all right. It's all right. You lived. You did well."

She and Maggie laughed and laughed.

"The bear's balls. You touched his . . ." Maggie chortled and they both folded over, rocking gently, almost crying, trying to say the word "testicles."

Maggie touched the bandages over her own face and said, "Uh oh. The doctor's gonna yell at me again." Blood began to freckle the bandages. Maggie assumed a stern expression, shook her finger back and forth and said, "Margaret Johnson, no more laughing. Do you hear? No more smiling."

Sometimes Maggie and Beryl got quiet. They sat side by side, not saying a thing.

Every once in a while one of them would jump slightly at a movement in the window, the wind in the snow or a nurse all in white running to the cafeteria. They both watched the movement until the end, conscious of their own breath.

Beryl looked over at Maggie then. She faced the hard bandages, the plaster nose pushed out as if sniffing, the swirl of white, the small black eye. She expected Maggie to yawn and show a black tongue, sharp teeth.

The experience had changed Maggie. She said she hadn't been stupid like Beryl and lost her way. She'd known where the hotel doors were, had stepped out of the car toward them. But then the white mass she'd thought was part of the hotel wall had knocked her right back against the car. The strange part was, she said, when the bear had reached forward with its mouth open for the front of her parka, she'd relaxed. Like the bear was going to give her a backrub. Her muscles just loosened. She'd felt the pressure, the tugging, but she'd been peaceful, very aware and far away.

She ran her hand round the edge of her bandages and said, "You're going to think this is really weird of me. But it was one of the best moments of my life."

She said she no longer got scared out on the patrols, turning alone outside in the snow. She felt warm then.

Beryl turned back to the window, away from Maggie. She moved her hands. She had problems now staying still. At night she wanted to wander down the halls, white floors, white walls, the smell of the wind and floor cleaner rising up beneath her, leading her toward the door.

The tall doctor told Beryl the risks. Where the skin had frozen once, it could easily be frostbitten again. The circulation had been damaged. Her toes especially would always need protection. Everyone had areas of bad circulation, and some people are more susceptible to frostbite. She couldn't be exposed for long. She could lose fingers, the rest of her toes, her nose. The doctor looked down severely at Beryl, lying in bed. He wore a white lab coat, carried a white clipboard. Beryl found herself wondering what he thought of all this white in his life.

The doctor asked her what kind of clothing she had for the cage. Beryl looked down at her hospital gown and the bandages. She recited the *Natural Photography* list.

"Yes," he said, "yes." He nodded. "That's good. But never more than twenty minutes."

"Yes," Beryl said, "yes." She had no intention of wearing the *Natural Photography* suit again. She thought if she had been able to move more easily she could have kept warmer, if her vision hadn't been so restricted by the hood she might have been able to find her way back.

The day before they left, the doctor took off the bandages. Beryl's feet had been the least prepared for the cold. She hadn't worn the electric socks, just five pairs of wool. She thought maybe the circulation had partially been cut off by all the material. She examined her feet slowly, carefully. In outline they now reminded her of cartoon feet, like the Flint-stones', only the big toe and three others. So much simpler, three such a magical number. She tried to imagine wear-ing sandals again or standing barefoot by a pool. Someone staring at her feet, knowing something was wrong, but not sure what. She imagined, in the heat of the sun, by the blue glare of the pool, trying to explain. She remembered rocking forward through the storm. She felt again the strength rising in her limbs.

Her feet were peeling; white patches of dead skin stuck out

across her toes, ankles, soles. The patches peeled off easily, pink skin beneath. A scab lay where each of her little toes used to be. The smallness of the scabs surprised her a bit, the exact circumference of her old digits. She'd had many bigger scrapes on her knees as a kid. She pressed her thumbs into the empty place where her flesh used to be. It felt as if her toes were still there, curled in, pressed tight against her feet.

She pulled her hands away. Her body had grown smaller, losing weight once again. There would be more space within her shoes, a small pucker for an extra fold of socks to fill.

She eased her feet out of the bed and stood up slowly. The weight shifted more onto the outside of her arches. She'd never been conscious before of her baby toes, never really noticed them, yet now the lack of them pushed her legs out just a touch to compensate. She stepped forward, holding on to the bed, rolling slightly, cautious. Her feet didn't leave the ground all the way. She shuffled, her arms held out, her head up. As she had in the storm, as awkward as a newborn.

She looked down triumphant.

For a moment she thought she saw white patches of fur growing out from her ankles.

CHAPTER 17

They left on Monday morning, five days behind schedule, on the morning the bus arrived. *Natural Photography* had had the Arctic Traveler designed for the expedition in hopes of selling a whole line of them to the companies that maintained the Trans-Alaska Pipeline. The first thing that struck Beryl when she saw the bus was its vast black tires. They stood easily eight feet high, wider than she was tall and with tread deep enough to swallow her whole fist.

Butler slapped his hand against the tires as affectionately as against a horse's neck. "There's no air inside these babies. Air would contract too much at the first real chill. They're not even made of rubber. Some sort of new compound of Mylar and metal." Looking closer, Beryl saw that the tires had a light silver shimmer, like a puddle with oil in it. "They've been tested in cold down to eighty below," Butler continued.

"With tires this wide the bus can hump its way up a mountain of ice."

He crouched slightly to point out a network of tubes and cylinders curving beneath the high belly of the bus. Some of the tubes looked as if they were made from the same material as the tires, but the cylinders were made of a light metal. The whole thing looked as complex as the exposed innards of an animal. The bus stood so high on its tires Beryl could have crossed beneath if she walked with her head tilted just a bit to the side. Even on four legs, the bigger bears would have to crawl to get under the bus, their front legs held out as they shuffled forward.

"There's a holding tank for waste," Butler said, pointing. "It's carried along under here so we don't dirty up where we travel. Very environmental and all. It's used as insulation for the main gas tank." Butler pointed farther back. "There's even an extra safety tank with enough fuel for fifty miles or five days of heat, whichever you prefer."

Above them the bus hunched heavy, a metallic lime green. Beryl wondered if the green was a misguided attempt to make visitors from temperate zones feel more at home. Butler swung open the doors, which hissed and sighed just like those on a Greyhound bus.

Holding them back for a moment with his arm across the doorway, Butler smiled at them and said, "You know, I don't want you thinking this is going to be roughing it in any way. I'm talking a VCR, microwave, stereo. This thing's so spacious it's really our little arctic RV. Arctic RV, don't you like that? We've got a Kelsey generator—the size of a V-8 and twice as efficient. We can afford to be comfortable." The four of them would share four hundred square feet for the next three weeks. On weekends they would make the three-hour trip back into Churchill to take a break from each other. The project would be done whenever the ice froze and the bears stalked away across it.

The bus's engine was in the front, beneath the driver's seat. When they started it up, the vehicle heaved into motion, rumbling and groaning, making normal conversation difficult in the front room. The scenery moved by very slowly. Jean-Claude drove and Butler sat happily in the passenger seat, studying the instruction manual and yelling out every feature of the bus and the corresponding set of directions. Beryl thought Butler had probably gotten hold of his first car long before he was legally allowed to drive, simply for the pleasure of taking the engine apart, tracing the insides of each of its components, and putting it back together again. When Butler pointed out an instrument on the dashboard, his hand ran over the object as though stroking a prize pet.

For each new feature essential to the bus's operation, Jean-Claude glanced at the diagrams available, asking questions until he was sure he understood. He shook his head over the extras that Butler seemed so pleased with. Beryl looked outside. The thermometer registered eighteen below.

David and Beryl decided to explore further. Behind the front room, which served as a living/dining/driving room, lay the kitchen and bathroom. Each room hummed busily with details designed to create a plush and comfortable look: hand-spun rugs glued to the floor, imitation wood paneling, calming colors that discouraged feelings of isolation and surging helpless fear. The rooms were eight feet tall, and Beryl noticed that every inch was put to use. In the kitchen pots hung from the ceiling above the oven. Everything had its place, locked in with an audible snap. Already Beryl wanted to move things around. She remembered the science museum exhibit of the square yard of space, tried to imagine this bus shrunk even further. Her imagination failed.

In the kitchen David and Beryl shuffled around each other opening cupboards and drawers, prying at the pictures glued onto the wall. In the tiny space they moved almost as closely together as they had when photographing bears from the van. She reached in front of him to pull at the toaster nailed to the counter. He put a hand on the top of her head to hold it safely out of the way while he opened a cabinet door above her. As on a ship, the plates and glasses had their exact places. Velcro nets fastened around the glasses and small prongs held the cups. The cupboards below were packed with every type of preserved food she could imagine—artichoke hearts, jars of pesto, mandarin oranges, tamarind concentrate and hoisin sauce. Cooking and eating were two of the few pastimes possible on board; the bus's designers had planned to make them as enjoyable as possible.

Opening the cupboards at face level, Beryl noticed she was leaning most of her body against David and that his hand had slipped down to comfortably cradle the back of her neck.

He was rummaging through the spices muttering something about Scotch peppers. She felt no tension at being this close, only the physical comfort of another body. She knew at some point the expedition would be over. The four of them would separate. They would make promises of reunions, future expeditions, but in the end they would leave the others and the Arctic and go back home. She would find another freelance job in the city. A few months later she would get a complimentary video of the show created from their trip. She would take it to her parents' house to show them, to explain her experience, but she would find that her story wasn't on the video. The four team members would hang back, invisible. Only the bears would be seen, stalking slowly through a world without people or arctic buses.

"Yugh," David said, pulling down a plate from the cupboard. "What is this shit? I think Holiday Inn and Hallmark cards designed this place." On the plate was the picture of a dewy-eyed, twig-legged fawn sitting up in a pile of leaves, one leaf still perched on its head. "Hell, these are the kind of people who think childhood is cute and restful."

Beryl pulled down another plate. The material felt light and cheap. The design showed a young woman walking on a beach at dawn, everything colored pink or beige. The wind pushed the woman's clothes against her front, outlining her breasts. The individuality of her face was erased by her hair. Beryl saw the men this plate was designed for, eating off it, uncovering her body with each mouthful. She dropped the plate back onto the counter. It bounced.

"Hey," said David. "Neat-o." He dropped the Bambi plate on the counter. It bounced back almost up into his hands. "This stuff is unreal. It's made for big engineers. I bet it's made from Mylar and metal too. If we get a flat tire we can strap these on." He dropped the plate onto the floor. It made a sharp click and bounced almost up to his knees. He caught it, whipped it at the floor. It came right back up into his hands.

"When I was a kid," he said, "I was definitely one of those who tested the claims of products: 'unbreakable,' 'stainless,' 'waterproof.' I figured it was an express invitation to me, personally. Once I left my watch for three days at the bottom of my aquarium before it finally filled up and stop working. All the numbers peeled off and floated to the inside of the glass face. Really, quite a neat-looking watch. I wish I had it now. Then, it bummed me out. I wrote a depressed letter to the manufacturer talking of my broken trust and decreased belief in the assurances of adults." He picked up a glass and dropped it straight down. It twacked against the floor and turned in the air. "He sent me a better watch free.

"Yo," he continued, "watch this." He pushed up his sleeves, reached for two more plates and began to juggle. He had skill, but the kitchen was too restricted for the plates to achieve more than a small arc. They kept bouncing off the edge of the cabinets or the hanging pans and spinning in ways David didn't expect. The plates hit him on the nose and shoulder and one hit Beryl on the ear. She held her hands out in front of her face and narrowed her eyes nervously.

"And now," David said while scooping another pile of

plates from the cupboard, "for the rarely tried and never accomplished triple somersault while juggling an entire setting for eight, including soup bowls. Ladies and gentlemen, silence please. This has the potential to be pretty embarrassing." Beryl watched amazed as David tossed the plates straight up into the air, where they clattered against the hanging pots and the walls and the cupboards. He immediately bent over to attempt a somersault toward the hall, but he seemed to have forgotten how, and his head got in the way as he tried to roll over on his shoulder. The bowls bounced off every surface around him.

He had balanced partway over on his shoulder and head, as though he were about to do a headstand, when Butler stepped into the doorway of the kitchen and thundered out, "What the hell's going on here?" Butler looked down at David's butt and stepped back quickly. Beryl thought he couldn't have looked more alarmed if David had been nude.

Butler retreated into the front room. "Try to keep it quiet," he blustered over his shoulder.

David stood back up, and he and Beryl looked at each other. He shrugged and they picked up the dishes.

Past the kitchen, they found the storage areas followed by the sleeping area: two bunk bedrooms on each side, one upper, one lower. Beryl crawled into one, dragging her luggage in behind. It reminded her of an animal's den. A complete room four feet tall with a door she could close for privacy and a dresser built into the wall. She couldn't imagine Butler trying to dress himself within its confines. She sat down in the center of her room. It was almost the size of her cage.

She put her clothes into the drawers without respect for neatness or order. She wanted this place to feel homey, human. Her socks stuck out of the top drawer. She took a picture of her parents out of her bag. It'd been taken by her father using a timer. He'd gone through two rolls of film trying to get the timing and angle right. In all the pictures he'd either been caught halfway to the chair in awkward positions of fast movement, or he'd been sitting in the chair looking expectant and slightly confused. In this picture of both her parents, her father was blurred and only just looking up from the seat he'd taken. Her mother simply looked patient, still, like an old-time frontier woman with one hand on the shoulder of her man.

Beryl tacked the picture to the wall facing where her head would be when she lay down, then changed it so they looked out the window to the whiteness. Her mother wore a summer dress in the picture. She wore sandals. Leaning close, Beryl could count all of her mother's ten toes.

Above she could hear David unpacking his clothes and closing the drawers. She heard him lie back onto the bed. The springs creaked with his weight. She heard a pause. He sighed.

Ten minutes later, David had fallen asleep. Beryl pulled on his ankle. "Grab your camera and parka," she said. "We still have the observation deck to see." The deck was an unheated glass room on top of the bus. The bus's designers said that on average it would stay twenty degrees warmer than outside. Beryl wore Jean-Claude's Inuit suit. She thought she could test it out in the cold of the deck.

She climbed up behind David's boots. When he opened the hatch to the deck, he gasped. She didn't know if it was from the cold or something else.

Sticking her head over the edge, she moved from the world of confines, small things and color schemes to the world of immense blue-white beauty. Snow was falling. Rolling ground receded into a distance hard to comprehend. The horizon curved gently out, smooth as the lip of a bowl. Closer in, ice walls stood up at broken angles. The puddles beneath them lay black and deep.

Churchill was a slight smudge hanging on the horizon behind them, a frozen gray cloud. Space out here was misleading, perspective difficult to grasp, the scale inhuman. She could have been looking across the breadth of the planet. She could have been looking across the landscape of a single cell.

Snow fell slow and graceful as the universe's spin. David and Beryl raised their cameras to their eyes without a word and began to shoot.

After a few photographs, she noticed the cage tied up on the roof behind them. It hunched dark, heavy-looking and small. The cage had seemed much larger when she'd first seen it, contained within a room. Here it sat hard and compact in a world white and open, like a squat creature from a dream, the kind that lumbered after her as she windmilled away even slower, trying frantically for the speed that she could only dimly remember.

Within ten minutes on the observation deck they saw their first bear. At first she thought the white world had come alive. A boulder stood up, stretched, then moved slowly across the barren plain toward them. It gained slowly. Curious, investigating. She couldn't yet see the movement of its black nose.

She and David went back down to have lunch. Her toes and hands felt numb. She moved carefully on the ladder, trying not to show the heavy uncertainty of her feet, the weakness of her hands. She went to her room, took her boots off. Everywhere on her feet she'd had frostbite, her skin hummed with a speed like heat, like cicadas on a hot summer day. She realized the difference between this cold and the kind she'd been used to in the States. There, when she went outside, even for the whole day skiing in a bad crosswind, nose running and face red, the center of her still remained quite warm. Here, she felt a deep cold. She shivered and shivered. Long after her skin had warmed up, the cold inside her wouldn't go away. Still, she was impressed with the Inuit suit; the other suit had done as badly even inside the protection of a heated car.

The scabs from her little toes had broken open and bled, probably from walking around, moving her feet around in her shoes. She washed the blood off, put on new bandages, her fingers awkward and thick. It hurt less than she would have imagined. She slowly walked the twenty feet to the dining room, trying to put her feet down more gently, to ease them into each step. Already she walked with a bit of a sway.

CHAPTER 18

When she tasted the roast beef at lunch, she felt like she'd never eaten meat before, had just realized she was a carnivore. She felt a hunger that overwhelmed her. She wolfed another bite and another. The beef tasted rich like chocolate cake, satisfying like wine. She felt as if beef were the thing she'd been thirsting for her entire life. She swallowed a small curl of fat and it tasted so good she gobbled down the rest of it before continuing with the meat. At home she ate only beans and vegetables, bread and rice. Red meat had frequently made her feel sick, constipated. Now she ate it with a feeling near to starvation. She reached for a second helping.

Everyone was looking at her.

"That's a lot of food for a little tuck like you." Butler tilted his head to look at her with one eye closed. "Don't have a bun in the oven, do you?"

The others looked at him.

"I'm just kidding," he said. "Gawd."

Jean-Claude shook again with his soundless laugh. "She's learned fat is how you stay warm up here. That's how the Inuit do it. Up to ten pounds of seal blubber or caribou a day. Plenty of water too." He turned to her. "Make sure you drink water. The livers of the Inuit are swollen with toxins like basketballs. David should eat that much too. He's going out there."

David looked repulsed. Sitting beside him, Beryl saw his hand reach down to touch his flat belly.

"No." David shook his head. "I'm a vegetarian." His hand probed his gut, searching already for expanding organs.

Beryl continued to eat.

At two o'clock they arrived at the sea. They actually drove a little out onto it, but the snow was suddenly so choppy that David, who'd been driving while Jean-Claude went to the bathroom, stopped to ask his advice about which way to go next.

Jean-Claude backed up the bus as fast as it could go. Once they were on even ground, he stopped and pointed back to where they'd been. Water was already pooling in over their tracks. They could now make out the open sea eighty feet beyond that, a white solid kind of water Beryl had never seen before. With each wave the water bobbed up and down like a heavy plastic sheet. A thick mist rose from the waves and formed a solid wall of steam nearly sixty feet into the air.

"Arctic mist," Jean-Claude said. "The air is cold. The sea is warmer."

By this time four bears were following them. The bears stopped, uncertain, thirty yards back. Noses up, heads moving from side to side, they circled steadily closer to join the three bears already there—one rolled over with its stomach exposed like a huge cat sleeping, another strolling and a third sitting patiently at the edge of the solid ice. They looked to Beryl like people spending the day at the beach, passing time. When the bus had approached, all of them turned, heads up.

From inside the parked bus David and Beryl spent some time picking a location for the cage. They wanted a good view in all directions so they could film the bears on their own level without the telephoto, get the bears as they naturally lived. They delayed setting up the cage until the next day in hopes that the bears would have accepted the bus by then and wandered away far enough for them to move the cage to its location.

They didn't have much to do until morning, so David watched some of the videos that came with the bus's VCR. It was impossible to pick up any TV channels so far out, so they had to rely on prerecorded shows—movies, sports events and even old episodes of "Gunsmoke."

Butler turned on the stereo and listened to music with the headphones. Jean-Claude began to make dinner. Beryl noticed that they seemed quite comfortable being so close, within ten feet of one another, without talking. She found their attitude awkward, like being in a subway car with the people staring fixedly at the posters. She wondered if they were able to ignore one another this easily now, what would be happening in another two weeks.

Beryl got dressed and went up on the deck again. She could smell the sea along with the subtle musky scent she knew so well. Sitting in the half-dusk, she could not see how many bears were out there. She could only vaguely make out their lumbering shadows below. They paced in and out of the dark around the bus, looking up at its windows. They leaned against its sides and stretched upward with their paws. They crawled under one side and came out the other. One bear at the back of the bus spotted her and crouched repeatedly, swaying its head up and down to gauge perspective and distance. When it jumped, she simply held her breath. The animal hit the bus somewhere below her. The entire bus resonated. The bear staggered away, dazed.

The bears seemed to be more daring out here, as if they knew, away from town, that humans were the trespassers. Perhaps also, Beryl thought, the bears that went into town were the weaker ones, the ones who needed an easier meal from the dump or an abandoned house. The bears here had never scrounged for food, had never run from an encounter with a human, had never been darted with a tranquillizer and handled like interesting merchandise. These bears were the real things.

Jean-Claude came up to the observation deck. He sat

down beside her, his shoulder against hers. "David found some canned pears. He's making tarts for dessert. Dinner's almost ready," he said. She enjoyed the feeling of weight and warmth against her shoulder. "This is strange for me," he said, "being out here in a heated bus. Before I've always been on a snowmobile or sled."

She couldn't imagine slogging forward through this white desert, dogs yipping, throwing themselves against the harness. Without landmarks, she couldn't imagine picking any one place to bed down at night. Or see herself lying there, listening to herself and her dogs breathe upward, the only movement audible for miles.

They looked for a while out at the world. She could hear what was probably a bear chewing on the edge of a tire below.

She turned to Jean-Claude, touched his cheek with her glove and then reached forward to kiss him. Again she smelled his fresh wood smell. She tasted his lips, cold and surprised.

He pulled away, looked out at the landscape for a moment, then turned to her and kissed her back.

She pulled him closer. He tried to touch her face. His mouth felt warm. The skins between them rustled.

Someone thumped on the hatch. They jumped. Dimly they heard David yelling from below, "Dinner's ready."

She pulled back. Over Jean-Claude's shoulder she could see a huge bear yellowed with time, thirty feet away. It paced back and forth watching them, its flat head snaking about.

· · ·

At dinner she caught David's speculative glance. She blushed a bit under his gaze. When no one else was looking he narrowed his eyes, then wiggled his eyebrows suggestively. His face was so mobile, it could be the very mask of lewdness. She looked away, could feel the giggles welling up inside, tried to think only about cutting up her meat. Butler looked up from his dinner in time to catch David smiling widely at her reaction. Butler looked around the table, uncertain what was happening.

"The first time I met my present love was three years ago in court," David said. He leaned a little closer to Beryl and added, "We live together even now. It's a long-term thing. It's so nice not to be considered just some cheap love slave." Beryl wouldn't look at David. She was scared she would laugh. Jean-Claude wouldn't look up at any of them. He had two high spots of color in his cheeks. Rebuffed by the others, David began to address his remarks to Butler.

"Anyway, I was in court for running a stop sign, only there was no stop sign there. I had pointed that out at the time to the police officer, but he hadn't seemed all that interested. Chris was there to lend emotional support to a friend fighting a no-left-on-red rap. When it was time for Chris's friend to defend herself, she couldn't even stand up and so Chris did, giving this impassioned speech. From the moment I first heard that voice, I was in love."

Beryl noticed that at no time did David slip and reveal a gender. Sitting beside Butler, he leaned in closer, smiling, involved in his story. Butler looked around confused, then a little nervous. He leaned away from David, closer to Beryl. His knee touched her thigh. She crossed her legs, shifting closer to Jean-Claude.

"I congratulated my true love after the speech and, well, we spent the night together. We've been living together ever since." To emphasize the point, he touched Butler on the hand. Butler jumped. David looked startled, then something else moved across his face, something harder. Beryl watched him reach out deliberately to touch Butler on the shoulder. "Feeling a little tense?" he asked.

Butler leaned away. David looked for a moment at his hand hanging in the air between them.

For the rest of the meal, David stared at Butler and occasionally slid his chair closer in order to reach food on that side of the table. He bumped their shoulders together. Butler ducked his head down, turned away. His face reddened like a bashful girl. David smiled a hard lopsided smile.

She knew Butler's anger would be terrible.

When she was sure the others were asleep or at least should be, she tiptoed to Jean-Claude's bunk. She touched his bare shoulder. He awoke instantly. She could hear the slight change in his breath. He sat up, rubbed his eyes and awkwardly reached forward to touch her face. They returned to her bedroom because Butler slept above Jean-Claude's room; if David heard he wouldn't care as much. She pulled Jean-Claude's body after her into her bunk, closed the door.

She held him close. He seemed confused about what to

do. She wondered if he was uncertain because of his youth or because he met few women on these expeditions. Maybe he knew no one well. He was gentle and awkward. He sighed softly in surprise.

They weren't sure how the sound might carry. They breathed as deeply as in sleep, their movements slowed to the restlessness of dreaming. His body smelled sweet as cedar. He was slight and hard, made only of bone and sinew. Beryl thought he wouldn't change much in age, no fattening or shrinking. He would change little even in death, just a slight stiffening.

Afterward he cried. Like his laugh he made no sound as he cried, just his slight rocking breath and the water on her shoulder. She pulled him closer into her side.

In the morning when she awoke, she was alone.

CHAPTER 19

"Hey Butler," David said at breakfast. "You know, that turtleneck is just the perfect color for you." He smiled at Beryl and raised his eyebrows in anticipation of Butler's response.

Butler wouldn't look up from his cereal. He said, "It's just a shirt."

"But it's sea bottle green. It brings out your eyes," said David. Beryl was surprised that he could undertake this baiting of Butler so lightly.

Butler stirred his cereal around and around. Some of the flakes began to break up. "Hey Jean," he said, pronouncing it like "Gene," "why don't you tell us about the worst time you've ever had out here?" He smiled up at Jean-Claude, enthusiastic for this new topic. "Tell us about the last time you went out and everyone didn't make it back."

Jean-Claude put his toast down, looked at Butler and then around the table at the others. They were silent, watching him. Beryl realized she wasn't the only one who had wondered about the bad things that could happen on this journey.

Jean-Claude seemed confused by their interest. "Those times," he said slowly, "weren't comic books, not *stories*. People died. People I knew." He got up from the table. "Excuse me," he said and left.

Butler looked embarrassed. "I didn't think he would . . ." Beryl noticed that when he was upset his mouth hung soft and unbalanced; his face didn't look so guarded. "Look, I've got some notes to finish up." He left, carrying his dishes.

David and Beryl sat there for a moment. "Whew," said David. "Tension, tension."

Beryl laughed nervously and took another sip of her coffee.

David leaned back in his chair to see if anyone was coming around the corner. He pulled his chair a little closer to her and lowered his voice. "Now," he said, "while we've got a private moment, I'm going to be a busybody. I don't want to offend you or anything, but I gotta say it's not a good idea to be sleeping with anyone while we're locked up on this bus. I've seen this happen before with small groups. Once in Borneo, six days out from the nearest town, one guy almost killed another, knocked him down and hammered on his head with a steel water canteen. This bus is just too small, you know? It's gonna cause problems."

She felt the heat rising up her neck. She'd thought they'd been quiet enough. She got up to take her dishes to the kitchen. "I really think it's none of your business," she said.

He followed her and she turned to face him, standing close within the small kitchen. "Look," he replied, "normally, I would be the first to agree. But you don't know what can happen. You haven't seen it. It'll affect all of us."

"Well, speaking of a small bus," she asked, "what are you doing with Butler, huh?"

"Oh, come on." David looked startled. "That sort of shit he's doing pisses me off. Acting like I'm contagious. This is an education for him. If there were any justice in the world, he'd be paying me."

"You're scaring him out of his mind. That's really gonna make for a small bus."

He watched her. She could smell the mint from his toothpaste. He blinked.

"OK," he said. "OK. Let's you and me not start in on each other too. Let's keep our sense of humor about this stuff. Tell you what, I'll back off of Butler. And I suggest you back off of Jean-Claude. It's gonna be a long trip."

After breakfast Butler took to standing even closer to Beryl than before. He brushed up against her more than he had to, made sure to seat himself next to her at every meal, touched her waist when he needed her attention. He held a lock of her hair at one point, brought it to his nose, asking what shampoo she used. She leaned away, gritting her teeth.

That day she sat in the cage.

They took most of the morning figuring out a way to drag it to the right spot and get her in safely. They had assumed that the bears would lose interest and back off enough for them to maneuver the cage around. But the bears still prowled about the bus, even more of them than the night before. They explored the outside of the bus with a single-minded determination, bony with hunger. Many of them hadn't eaten at all in a month, hadn't eaten well in four months. This hunger didn't affect them as much as it would humans. When rearing young, the mothers sometimes went three months without touching food, emerging from their dens emaciated and desperate once the cubs had grown big enough to survive outside.

To drive the bears away from the bus, Butler first tried opening the front door just enough to shoot a gun into the air. The gun boomed across the snow, the echo shivered into the sky. The animals looked over, slightly curious. Butler handled the gun with an expert's ease, breaking open the chamber to load it. He aimed lower, closer to the bears. They looked up at the soft *whiz* of the bullet over their heads. None moved away. Butler shot the gun into the ground near their feet. They stepped forward to sniff the hole in the snow. Butler cursed.

He tried flares next, set them off and rolled them onto the snow. The smoke billowed out. The bears snorted, rubbed their noses in the snow and coughed. They moved upwind of the flares and sat down to wait.

Standing behind Butler, Beryl heard the bear before she saw it. A displacement in the air, breathing, the thud of snow. She couldn't see where it was coming from. Butler slammed the door shut. They heard a grunt from outside, some sliding. Silence. Butler swore at them all.

Jean-Claude finally tried plain noise. The bus had been supplied with several old and calming records: Willie Nelson, Frank Sinatra, the Osmonds. He played an old Osmonds record at the highest volume and broadcast it using the microphone hooked to the outside speakers. The noise rolled out, horrific, with a feedback squeal. It boomed out into the land of shifting silence, of barren winds and the creaking of ice. "AND THEY CALLED IT PUP-PY LO-HA-HA-OVE." The bears shook their heads, swiveled their ears and laid them down flat. One by one they began to move uneasily away.

Butler and Jean-Claude dragged the cage to the spot they had picked out forty feet from the bus. They half-ran, breathing raggedly in the cold. The bears stood a hundred yards away, nothing between them and the people. Carrying her camera equipment, Beryl followed the two men. She wore Jean-Claude's suit again. The fur shifted easily against her skin with each movement. She felt almost nude. The fierce cold startled her lungs each time she inhaled. Still, inside the suit she remained fairly warm.

The music continued to play. The noise outside felt all wrong—music meant for small rooms, heat and crowds, smoke and confines, thin summer clothing. This place was too large, too white. The words got distorted by the wind. This place was meant for deep silences and the fierce howls of storms a hundred miles wide.

Jean-Claude and Butler stopped, looked all around and

dropped the cage. No difference between this spot and the next. The men ran back. Beryl looked around at the bears. It would take them ten seconds to cover the distance to her, she thought. She pulled hard to open the cage door, then harder, before she realized the latch was turned. She opened it quickly and got in. Closed the door, locked it by twisting the two bars in two different directions at the same time. It took a moment for her gloves to get traction on the steel, to turn the bars correctly. The designers had assured her that this type of lock couldn't be opened by mistake, couldn't freeze shut. She hoped her hands would stay warm enough to unlock it.

She put her cameras with their heaters down in front of her, the extra gloves, the walkie-talkie. She organized the cameras, the Nikon closest, then checked the lock again.

She swung with all her weight on the lock, testing it just to make sure. Stretched her legs out one last time, then tucked them back in. The music died with a squeal as Jean-Claude closed the bus door.

She sat in the cage. It fit as she'd imagined.

The bears sniffed the air and trotted slowly in.

She could hear their methodical breathing, the thump of their feet approaching through the snow. Their heads held low, they trotted directly toward her. She could feel the cold creeping up her legs and across her buttocks, which pressed against metal. She ignored it. She wanted to stay out here for at least ten minutes.

She forced herself to put a camera up to her eye, to shoot,

saw the thick metal bars of the cage define the approaching bears. The big yellow bear Beryl had spotted last night
ran forward ahead of the others, her mouth open. Beryl had
never seen the bears from ground level, sitting down. They
were huge, as tall as a standing person but wider. They ran
easily toward her, their fur rolling loosely, their heavy paws
slapping forward. She wanted to stand up, to run away from
them. She tasted bile in the back of her mouth. The big female
didn't slow down as she got close. Her shoulder hit the bars.
The whole cage rocked back. The bear grunted. Beryl's skull
slapped back against the bars. She felt a reverberation in her
head like something wooden hit hard. Beryl pulled herself
forward quickly, away from the bars, a high-pitched hum in
her ears.

The bear's heavy head swung up over the top of the cage
and looked down at Beryl. The bear sniffed the metal. She
tried to push her snout in. Her massive body filled Beryl's
vision. Seated, Beryl felt even smaller. The thick white fur of
the bear's chest stuck though the bars in front of her. Hesitantly, Beryl reached one hand out to touch the fur, took a
picture of her small black glove against the white tufts of the
chest. She was in the cage. Her head hurt.

The bear coughed in shock at her touch. Her breath, animal and warm, brushed Beryl's face. She brought her head
down and looked at Beryl straight on, eye to eye. Beryl could
see the bear's pinkish tear ducts, just like a child's. Every
hair on Beryl's body stood up with a prickling sweat. Even as

it happened, she knew this would be the moment she would remember just before she died. She could feel the cold penetrating slowly from her fingers to her arms. She didn't care anymore.

She touched the parka over her collarbone. The skins rustled with each breath she took, the breath on which she could taste the clear frozen air, the warm heat of the bears, the musky smell of wolverine fur, her own body.

The bear's nose moved, wet gleaming ebony skin, the curled inner tunnel shimmering a darker red. The black drawn-in smile of her mouth pulled back, opened, the inside dark as velvet, wet. Beryl realized she'd been moving her hand toward the nose. To touch it, to stroke the small slit openings for the eyes. She felt dazed. She pulled her hand back, checked her position again, tried to breathe more evenly. Her knees and elbows in, head down, no cameras within range of their paws. She placed both her hands on her camera, raised it again and looked at the bear through the lens.

The other bears approached cautiously from the sides and back. They panted, the only sound.

The large female stuck the front of her paw in between the bars. Only the claws and the first half of the front pad would fit. She fanned her long white claws at Beryl, like fingers gesturing her forward.

Beryl wanted to kiss each individual claw. She wanted to chew on the meat of the bear's toes.

. . .

The walkie-talkie crackled. "Hello, Beryl. Do you read me? Over."

She was trying to take a picture of a bear stretching his mouth open around two bars of the cage. The mouth filled her camera, black and wet, white curved teeth, long tongue. Her finger wouldn't work well enough to push the button. It just made aimless motions over the top of the camera. She'd stopped shivering a while ago. The bear's teeth tentatively touched the metal, a scraping sound. He sneezed, closed his mouth, stepped back. He sneezed again, sniffed at the bars.

Some of his saliva had already frozen on Beryl's feet.

"Beryl. Beryl, hello. Do you read? This is Jean-Claude. You all right? It's been half an hour. Do you read me? Thirty minutes. Over."

She put her camera down, looked back at the bus. It stood out, all wrong—shining green, metal, antenna, black tires. She picked up the walkie-talkie. Some sea ice cracked suddenly behind her on the shore, startling her. She could hear the waves now. They made a crunching sound, grating against the ice.

One young bear pulled herself onto the top of the cage. Her body blocked out the sun. The cage settled farther into the snow with a slow squeak. The bear moved around on top of the bars, looking down at Beryl, confused, determined. Her claws scraped against the metal, the pads of her feet pushing down around the bars. Beryl sat in the shade of the bear's body, looking up at the black padded feet the size of her head. She put the walkie-talkie back down, picked the camera up. Her hands fumbled. The camera fell back hard against the metal bars. The lens shattered. Picking up another camera, she watched her hands to make sure they closed. She tried focusing on the bear's face looking down between her feet.

"Beryl, don't worry. Beryl. We're coming."

The music began to play again. Feedback squeals. The bears snorted. The young bear jumped off the cage. They moved away, more slowly this time. Small figures ran toward her from the bus.

She looked at them curiously.

She snapped out of it soon enough. Once she was inside and her face had warmed up a bit, she tried to hide her lack of interest in the three men. She folded her face into gratitude. She told them the batteries in the walkie-talkie probably couldn't take the temperature. Her mouth moved heavy with cold, her words slurred as if she were drunk. Jean-Claude made a heater for the walkie-talkie.

She watched his hands moving, looked down at her own hands still within the gloves. She knew some of this distance was what Jean-Claude felt, why he moved so slowly and spoke in such short sentences.

She walked back to her room, stripped slowly. She lay in bed waiting for the feeling to return in her limbs, for the pain, the pulsing tingling itch. The second and third smallest toes on her left foot felt nothing. Soon they would begin to hum, then hurt. If she went out there several times for that long they might blacken, and fall off, like the rotten fruit from a tree. She would be smaller, paring down to her essence, two-toed, only hard calluses where the others had been. She wondered if it was possible to run without any toes at all. In the mirror she saw pale spots on her nose and cheeks.

She dozed, at peace in the silent emptiness of her room. She saw herself as parts: fingers, hands, feet, arms, facial features, all removable. She saw herself empty and free of them all, a pulsing envelope, organs, rhythmic and warm, unencumbered. She could trace her blood pumping through each section of her body, the beat pulsing differently in her hands and then her feet, as though she had several hearts like a worm.

Jean-Claude sat on the bed beside her, closed the door behind him. He checked her hands, her toes, her ears. She'd been close to frostbite, he said, on her toes and hands. He looked into her face. He shook her chin. He was telling her she must be more careful. He was telling her the cold came quick sitting still in a cage. No more than ten minutes out there from now on, he insisted. If she got any more frostbite, he would send her back to town. He wouldn't hesitate. If there were any complications she could get an infection, gangrene. He sounded worried. His hands moved into her shirt. He no longer touched her professionally. She responded languorously, rolling in against him as smoothly as a seal. Nothing remained in her mind but the immediate sensations of her body.

They heard footsteps approach down the corridor, stop

near her door. With her door closed, it was obvious where they both were. The person walked away. A moment later, Butler called from the front room that lunch was ready. Even muffled by the intervening walls, she could still hear the anger in his voice.

At lunch she felt high, far beyond the tensions of the three men about her. She ate meat and fat, packed it away. She wondered what animal the meat came from. When it had died, where.

No one talked to anyone. Butler left as soon as he had eaten. Jean-Claude touched her knee under the table. He reached across her for the salt, his nostrils flared near her shoulder.

After lunch, David got ready to get into the cage. Jean-Claude asked him if he wanted to wear the Inuit suit. David looked at the two simple layers. He said, "I'm sure the Inuit knew what they were doing when they designed that thing, but they just didn't have access to Thinsulate, you know?"

Jean-Claude tried to explain the benefits of the two skins, but David said, "Listen, I've followed the advice of *Natural Photography* for fourteen years now without a problem. I wouldn't want to start thinking things out on my own. Besides," he added with a grin, "I'm allergic to wolverine musk. It's not something most people would ever find out, but in my line of work . . ." He shrugged and zipped up his jacket.

David looked very small walking to the tiny cage across the massive white landscape. Even David's cameras seemed bigger than he was. They gleamed in the clarity of the air and the sun.

After the first three minutes Beryl couldn't even see David under the white shoulders and haunches of the bears. She wouldn't have known if the cage had broken open. She remembered scenes of lionesses feasting in the savannah, muted growling, teeth clenched, heads jerking back and forth.

Within five minutes David, trying hard to control himself, called in on the walkie-talkie. "My feet are fucking frozen." His voice sounded staticky and distorted over the radio, like a historical recording of a person long dead. "My legs have gone to sleep. I'm going to have to stretch them soon. They'll bite my toes off and I won't even feel it. I'm a fucking frozen TV dinner out here."

In the background Beryl could hear something rhythmic, heavy, startling. The bears' breathing.

"Get me out," David said. "Now."

Jean-Claude put on the music. The bears fidgeted, snarled, turned around as if trapped, and then meandered majestically away. Butler made a joke, something about leaving David out there and frozen flowers.

Beryl didn't really listen. She was realizing that they wouldn't last three weeks out here.

CHAPTER 20

That night they played gin rummy. Beryl had problems holding the cards all together and upright. Her fingers tingled and quivered, jerked slightly. The skin of her face tickled as if cold water were running across it. Her mind, however, worked perfectly. Without trying she could remember each card that had been played. She could almost see the faces of the cards the others held. She won hand after hand. Butler's lip rose higher and higher until his teeth gleamed simple and white. David kidded that after this trip he would take her on the rummy circuit, manage her, train her. They would make millions.

When David said the words "after this trip," Beryl knew again that something would go terribly wrong. Things would get bad soon. Her scalp itched, her teeth tingled. She looked at the outside thermometer. It registered twenty-seven below.

She noticed Jean-Claude's hands again, knew the softness

with which they could move. She saw that Butler's hair was thinning back in an arrow over each temple and felt how scared he must be of his own body's changes. Her heart thumped and roared. She began to cry without even putting down her cards, feeling quietly surprised. Only when it was her turn to pick up did the men see. They sat there stupidly, watching her until she found the strength to push herself up on her feet, swaying like an animal, and stagger slowly back to her room.

Behind her, she heard Jean-Claude say good night and follow her.

Butler said something softly about women and the outdoors and David said, "Maybe." The first time, she realized, she'd ever heard them close to agreement.

That night she cried onto Jean-Claude's chest and the sharpness of his ribs against her face made her wince with each subterranean thump.

The next morning she awoke late and went to the bathroom. The door was closed as always but not locked, so she walked in. In front of the mirror stood Butler naked, shaving. He turned quickly. The razor buzzed. He stood white and tall, round-bellied. For a moment she thought, He shaves his whole body and masquerades.

He sighed soundlessly and moved his hands to cover his nudity. The razor hummed black and metallic at his groin, as though he were about to urinate from it. In shock she barked a short laugh.

His look turned to pure fury.

"Oh god," she said, covering her mouth, "I'm sorry." She closed the door and walked to where David and Jean-Claude played rummy in the living room. She sat down in a chair and looked out across the huge white plain, her fingers rubbing the polished wooden arms of the chair over and over.

That afternoon it was her turn to go out again. Halfway to the cage, she had a sudden image of Butler wrecking the outside speakers or breaking the record player. She looked back to the bus.

By the time she'd closed the cage and locked it, she didn't care. The bears again. This time she allowed herself to close her eyes and simply listen to them coming for her: the squeak of snow, the swing of their weight. She wished she could take the sounds back with her. No cars, no other people, no other animals or movement, a world empty but for her and the bears and the creaking of a frozen sea.

A bear slapped hard against the bars beside her head. The metal twanged. The bear snorted, settled down onto the snow and begin to lick its paw. It sounded like a big dog cleaning itself. Without looking she knew it was the bear who had tried to chew the bars yesterday. He must be young, impatient, certain of his own power.

Beryl heard the sound of claws working at the snow. She opened her eyes. The big yellow female hunched in front of her, digging. Every few minutes she would push her head into the hole and reach up to touch the bars at the bottom.

This worried Beryl. She wouldn't be able to move her rump and legs off the floor of the cage without putting herself at risk from the top.

A bear levered patiently at the bars with her teeth. Slowly her tongue moved out to touch the bars. The bear screamed instant and shrill, jumped back five feet, black flesh left on the metal. The other bears sniffed the air suspiciously, looked about.

The yellow female, bored with digging, wriggled her paw through the cage in front of Beryl again, like a child at the zoo. Beryl leaned forward and smelled the black raspy pad of the paw. She ran her tongue over the claw: cool, salty, clean. The bear pulled it back, sniffed her paw.

Beryl leaned away, pushed her nose into the weight of the wolverine trim and breathed deeply, moving her tongue against her teeth, tasting the salt.

Reaching for her camera, she heard a low buzzing, looked about her on the ground. Nothing moving but the bears. She knew they couldn't make that noise. The hum got louder. She looked up: a bush plane headed into Churchill. It looked all wrong against the empty sky, the silent land, the bears lumbering slowly about beneath. It looked as awkward and fatal as a rock thrown hard. She wondered if the pilot could see her cage.

That second day, after her ten minutes in the cage, she found it more difficult to get warm. Even an hour after Beryl had returned to the bus, she shivered, her teeth chattered, her head hurt. Her limbs creaked and protested at each movement and felt heavy and dull. During lunch she tried to eat more meat and fat. She put on more clothing, drank warm liquids. She thought she must have spent too much time out there.

Then she noticed that everyone else seemed cold as well. They all wore more clothing. Jean-Claude wore two sweaters, Butler had on a scarf. David had even draped a blanket across his shoulders. It was now thirty below outside. Maybe the heaters weren't capable of dealing with this extreme.

That night while the rest of them played cards, Jean-Claude worked on the heaters and read again through the lengthy documentation on temperature control.

CHAPTER 21

The next morning she woke in the gray hour before dawn, exhaling cold white mist into the air above her bed. She drowsily watched the mist for a while without understanding, simply admiring the beauty of its dissolution. Then she awoke fully. Jean-Claude had rolled into a small ball completely beneath the covers. Her body moved stiffly. Her head hurt from the cold. She pulled herself out of bed without waking Jean-Claude, dragged her robe on and limped to the thermostat in the hall. It was set to heat the inside of the bus to fifty-five. The inside thermometer read thirty-eight.

She turned the thermostat up to seventy, held her hand over the heaters. Nothing. She looked out the window and saw three mounds of snow on the flat predawn plain about the bus. She knew each one contained a sleeping bear. She knew they would wake soon, shake off the snow, pace slowly along the ice. The sky was gray, the snow was gray. Nothing moved. The inside of the windows had frost on them. She scraped at a bit and it melted on her fingers.

She walked into the kitchen, turned on a burner. She heard a click somewhere in the stove and the electric coil began to heat. She smiled, relieved, held her hands over it for a minute. The coil blushed slowly, the red spreading out across its metal. She could hear the rhythmic breathing of the three sleeping men. The moment seemed so peaceful. She held her face down toward the burner, as though to smell the heat. It made such a difference to know the bus wasn't completely dead. Turning the burner off, she got back into bed.

She held Jean-Claude close for one slow minute more. Her face still felt warm. She pushed it into the scoop of his neck, smelling salt and sleep and a hint of last night's tomato soup, smelling everything clearly. She wanted this moment to last forever. The cold pressed down upon her.

She woke him up.

Jean-Claude checked several switches inside, then got dressed to go outside to check the tanks. Beryl dressed also. When she started to turn on the music, he shook his head. "Have to save the battery," he said. He handed her a rifle. The door opened with a hiss, like the transit buses in Boston. She thought for a moment she would step out onto Mass. Ave.: stores, traffic, people.

Outside nothing in all the flat gray moved. A perfect silence. She kept an eye on the snowy lumps of the bears. Soon they would be waking.

Beryl and Jean-Claude looked beneath the bus. Immediately they saw that all the Mylar pipes had been chewed through. In some places only shiny black shreds remained. The edges of the tires had been gnawed on. Even some of the metal had the bright scratches of teeth. Frozen spots of yellow vomit with black threads laced through it sprinkled the ground. Beneath the bus their fuel froze slowly in oily puddles, clawed footprints all about. At the back, the reserve tank had made a smaller puddle. The fuel stained the ice and snow beneath the surface of each puddle in a wide bowl, creating a shadowy impression of something half-alive and crouched. Nothing dripped out now. Their fuel was gone.

Beryl watched white heat roll from her mouth with each breath. The sky had soft touches of red. She stepped close to Jean-Claude, touched his arm. He didn't respond. They went back inside.

First they tried to call for help. The on-board radio crackled loudly with static. Jean-Claude put on the headphones and slowly twisted the dial, trying to find someone, his back hunched with concentration. His hands didn't move hesitantly now, as they had the night before. They moved smoothly, with determination. She wanted to go back to bed with him. She wanted to wake up again, to have it be warm.

Minutes passed with only static. Then the static began to get softer. Beryl watched Jean-Claude. He wasn't touching the volume control.

A man's voice suddenly boomed out of the speaker.

"Eh, now tha's really brilliant, Sammy," the voice said. "What's Marie think, eh? Over."

"Hello?" Jean-Claude spoke quickly into the microphone, each word crisp. "This is Jean-Claude Thibedeaux of *Natural Photography*'s Manitoba expedition. I need help. Do you read me? Over."

"Sammy, was that you? Over."

"Naw, Craig, you idiot, that's some guy calling from Quebec."

"Quebec? He said Manitoba, didn't he? I can barely hear him."

Jean-Claude looked confused. He leaned closer in over the microphone, began to shout. "This is Jean-Claude Thibedeaux of the *Natural Photography* Churchill expedition. I am in Churchill, Manitoba. I need help. Urgently. There are three others with me. Our bus is out of gas. Over."

"See, Craig, he's not from Quebec. He's from Manitoba."

"Shut up, Sammy. He's in trouble."

"Well, he should get hold of someone closer. Hey, Jean-Claude, this is fucking Saint John's. Go find a gas station in your own time zone. Over."

"Shut up, Sammy. Please continue, Jean-Claude. Please talk louder. Over."

Jean-Claude began to bellow. "I am forty miles east of Churchill, Manitoba. I am with the *Natural Photography* magazine. I am out of gas. We have no heat. We do not have the equipment to walk back. Please send help. Please contact the *Natural Photography* headquarters in New York City. Please contact Churchill police. Do you read me? Over."

There was a pause. Beryl had to lean closer to the speaker to hear them at all.

"Is he still speaking?"

"I can't tell. Did you get any of that?"

"I don't know. He's out of gas somewhere in Manitoba and he wants the church police. Something about photography. Over."

"Marie says he said something about 'photography bed quarters.' Did you get that? Over."

"Did she get anything else?"

"For Christ's sake, Craig. He's just out of gas. He's probably some fucking American tourist standing on a major interstate a thousand miles away. Get a life. Over."

"Jean-Claude, please repeat information. Please repeat information. Over."

The men couldn't hear Jean-Claude again, although he kept yelling until the radio wouldn't even hum and the bus's battery was completely dead. Jean-Claude found a hand-cranked emergency radio in the storage cupboard. He set it on the same frequency as before, began to crank fast and hard. His face had gone solid as ice, vacant as a bear's.

The outside thermometer read twenty-nine below. From the front of the bus Beryl could see six more polar bear mounds, their backs built up into round tents by the drifting snow. The cold of her face felt unreal. She hugged her parka tighter, wished she could have just one last cup of hot coffee, some warm soup. She held her breath, listening. Nothing, not even static.

Woken by the yelling, Butler and David appeared, standing in the hall holding blankets around them and breathing steam. They looked at her and Jean-Claude silently, eyes still puffy from sleep.

The temperature inside the bus had dropped to thirty-four. Jean-Claude suggested they all use the bathroom one more time before the water froze. Beryl felt like a small child departing on a family trip with everyone going to the bathroom before they left. The light in the bathroom wouldn't turn on. She crouched in the dark, the cold prickling the skin across her rear, trying hard to empty her bladder completely. Without the heaters on, they could hear so much better in the bus. They could all hear the fast stream of her urine. She could hear David in the front room asking, "But why's this happening? I've been on more than thirty expeditions. Nothing like this has ever happened before."

David cleared his throat, and she could see the way he would be holding his head to the side, sharp eyes looking about, mouth smiling. He would try to pretend this wasn't serious. "If this was going to happen," he continued, "why couldn't it happen on one of my nice warm Thailand expeditions? I mean why here and why during the start of winter? Why with large carnivores instead of the tree slugs in Venezuela?

"And while I'm at it, how could they have designed this

bus like that? Didn't they know the bears would do this?" No one answered. He said, "What a stupid question. I can't believe I asked such a stupid question. Not enough Mylar occurring naturally in their diet? Why doesn't someone else talk?" No one said a word.

When Beryl flushed, something in the pipes began to block. The water murmured up, puddled over. Jean-Claude turned off a valve on the main panel. The water stopped. The puddle on the floor began to harden. It smelled light and sharp in the cold. She walked into the front room and there they all stood, holding blankets around their shoulders, waiting.

Jean-Claude said, "We're going to have to walk back."

None of them looked at the others. Without the heaters and motors, the snowy silence from outside seemed to ease into the bus. A bear bumped somewhere underneath and they all heard the rustle of its hair against metal.

Butler nodded sadly. "Yeah, guess you're right."

Beryl examined the small decorated details of the bus and then looked out to the wide white space beyond. "OK," she said quietly, almost to herself.

David looked from one to another. "Aw, come on," he said. "What are you guys talking about?"

She turned into the kitchen to pack the food they would need. She felt much better now that she had something to do. The fridge sighed when she opened it and let out a breath of air warm in comparison to the cold room. They would be eating only meat on the journey, lots of it. Two days, three.

While she packed she ate the meat they had already cooked, ate quickly, efficiently, holding the slices in her gloves. She could feel the chill from the floor in her feet and ankles. When she had finished all the cooked meat she still felt empty, shivering. She looked at the raw meat. No way to cook it. It took her a while to cut off a slice with the knife, but her teeth went through each chunk keenly, easily. It tasted wet, cold. It left stains on her gloves.

The kitchen was dark. She could see the snow getting brighter outside. She heard Jean-Claude cranking the radio. Not even static.

She wanted to scream in fear. She wanted to dance in anticipation. She ate more meat.

They heard a low buzzing. For a moment she thought the heaters had come back on, the bus had sprung to life, the radio would work. They all looked up at the ceiling. "A plane," she said. "It's a plane."

She yelled to turn on the music, forgetting for a second that it wouldn't work. She ran outside, grabbing the flare gun over the doorway. She sprinted clear of the bus out into the snow, pointed the flare slightly ahead of the small bush plane, fired. The bright colors rustled up and across the sky—yellows, reds, smoke. The plane must have seen it.

The back of her neck itched. Slowly she looked to her left. A bear sat facing her forty feet away. It looked sleepy, snow still across his back. He sniffed the air. She put the second flare in. She knew it wouldn't kill the bear. It would only anger him. The animal and she faced each other. The plane continued straight along its path. She took a slow step back. Another. The bear stopped sniffing. His cheeks rolled back to show his teeth. He stood up. She couldn't check to see if there was another bear behind her. She couldn't turn her back on the bear's stare. She stepped back. Dark eyes, small eyes, focused. She turned and ran, heard again the sounds of a bear's claws through snow, its weight. No bars between them. She slammed the door behind her. The bear's body bounced off the outside. The metal creaked.

The temperature had dropped even further in the bus from the open door. The men were all leaning against the front windshield, watching the plane disappear.

CHAPTER 22

Jean-Claude gave them each a pair of snowshoes. He said to David, "I haven't had as good luck as you with the expeditions I've been on. I always bring backups."

He assembled a five-foot sled he'd brought. It had curved wood runners and a stretched hide platform. The pieces lashed together with strips of gray leather.

Butler said, "Hey, there are some nails in the tool chest. We could put that thing together tighter."

Jean-Claude shook his head. "The sled has to bump across the ice. Nails would shatter, crack open the wood. Narwhal's flexible. It allows the sled to twist." He stretched each lashing carefully over its post, flattening it with his fingers, pulling tight. The leather had light circular markings, like the rings of a honeycomb. Beryl hadn't known narwhals still existed. She couldn't picture one except from a seventeenth-century painting she'd seen; beneath the weight of its twisting horn,

189

the small whale pulled back red human lips and smiled. When Jean-Claude was finished he packed the blankets and radio.

With the fire ax Beryl broke up each of the dining-room chairs for wood to burn. She swung the ax hard in the small area. The wood cracked loudly. Splinters fell about. Her arms felt strong, her body heated up. The edges of the rug tore away from the corners of the room. Underneath she saw particleboard. She tied together the pieces of the chairs, working quickly and carefully. Her whole being concentrated on what they would need. For kindling she added the five books of bus documentation, their notebooks, the trip's journal. She and Jean-Claude broke the legs off the dining-room table. They packed it all tightly on the sled, balancing the weight carefully, lashing everything down. They wouldn't want to repack outside. Their hands wouldn't move as well out there.

Packing, they didn't have to say a thing to each other. They both understood. Her body was warm with work.

David watched them. He said, "I hate to disagree with you all, but I don't understand. It's still warmer in the bus." His lips looked blue. He wore every layer of clothing on the *Natural Photography* list, the parka's material straining, bloated with all the clothing beneath. He touched his lips with his gloves. "Why don't we wait for the plane? One went over yesterday, one went over today. Can't we sit tight here and hail it tomorrow?"

Butler faced him, impassive. "Both planes were heading into Churchill. If it's a daily flight and not just a coincidence, then it'll pass us tomorrow on the trail. We'll bring the flare gun. If not, then we don't waste a day in this cold."

David smiled weakly. "You know, I moved to California to get away from this kind of cold." He looked at each person in turn. He was the only one who still spoke conversationally, when he didn't have to. He stood by, watching them prepare. "Anyone have some Blistex?"

Butler cleaned the rifles. They had four of them, long and heavy. They swung open with soft clicks and well-balanced weight, wood and metal. Butler cleaned each of them carefully, loaded them, packed the ammunition. He put straps on the rifles and gave one to each team member.

It was eight in the morning. Normally she would have just woken up. Smelled hot coffee. Walked slowly to the bathroom in her bare feet, working the sleep out of her eyes with her fingers. She slung the rifle across her back. It rolled against her body, a solid weight.

They made a last quick check. Nothing left in the bus they needed. Every cupboard opened, all loose wood ripped up and packed. The clean, designed environment gone. It looked as if the bears had broken in already.

They stood in the front room and ate the last of the unpacked raw meat, standing, chewing, not talking. Their teeth made grinding noises. David only ate one bite. He grimaced at its texture. "I never liked steak tartare," he said. He threw the piece into the garbage. The other three turned to look at it.

David smiled. "A little fasting's good for everyone. Cleans

out the old system." He thumped his chest like Tarzan. "No one has any trail mix, huh?" The temperature in the bus registered twenty-seven. He wrapped his arms tight around himself. "You know, I can't tell you how serious you all look, like an ad to join the fucking army. Can't we take this with a little graceful groveling and fear? Can't we make some jokes?"

No one had much to say to that. Beryl touched the elbow of his jacket, smiled at him. She did not stop chewing.

Just before they left she went back to her room, put her favorite roll of film in the front pouch of her parka. She knew the film would freeze. But it would freeze on the bus anyway. She wanted it close to her. She left the picture of her parents, holding hands, on the wall facing out to the snow. Steam from her breath had already frozen to the edges of the picture and the window. Steam from when she'd been sleeping, still unaware.

Butler walked out first. With a quick swinging motion he shot two bears full in the face, giving the second bear no time to do more than jerk her head back. Both bears fell over. The reports echoed loud against the sky and the bus and returned several times. The other bears watched the two fall, then whirled and ran away. Beryl recognized one of the dead bears as the female whose tongue had gotten stuck to the metal. The other lay on his side with one palm extended, the young male who had stood on top of her cage, who had slapped the bars. The fur of both shivered a little and then stilled. The bodies lay heavy and white. Steam rose from the blood.

She wanted to lay her hand on the back of their wide flat skulls, to stand quietly by their side for a minute.

Jean-Claude and she lifted the sled down. It was heavy, a hundred fifty, two hundred pounds, a body between them. It cracked the skin of the snow when they set it down. They each put on their snowshoes and walked around the bodies. She found walking with the snowshoes awkward. She had to lift her toes up high, feeling like a heron. The wounds on her feet hurt for a while, then gradually numbed.

Butler led. He cradled the rifle across his body, in both hands, ready to jerk it to his shoulder and shoot. He held his head up higher than he had all week. He scanned for bears. He looked very tough except for the snowshoes, which gave him the exaggerated high step of Elmer Fudd.

David followed behind him. She could see the hood of his parka turning about as he looked for more bears. She couldn't see his face. The nylon made a raspy noise with each step forward. He stumbled as often as she did.

Jean-Claude walked beside her. They pulled the sled, the rope looped across their chests, like reindeer, like dogs. They walked forward, hand in hand. He moved slowly, smoothly. He wasted no motion. After a while their gloved hands let go, their fingers too cold to grasp.

She looked back over her shoulder. Their breath hung in the air behind and above them, gray and pall-like against the frozen blue of the sky. The bears were already ripping into the bodies. More bears trotted in from all over. More than she had imagined could be around.

The bears stayed behind with the fresh meat. They would have time to follow later.

After walking about twenty minutes, Beryl noticed that Jean-Claude was angling off to the left, while Butler walked straight on. Jean-Claude looked over at Butler. Twenty-five feet separated them before he stopped. "Butler," Jean-Claude said, "where you going? The inlet's that way." He had to raise his voice slightly because of the distance between them.

"What?" asked Butler, turning around. "Oh, come on. Going round'll cost us ten miles."

"It's too big a risk. The sled is heavy. We're heavy. Sea ice is hard to judge."

"Let's just try it." Butler was smiling. Beryl wondered if he'd ever been on an expedition that had gone wrong like this. She wondered if he'd always imagined how he would survive, how well he would do. She knew he had enjoyed shooting the bears, feeling at risk.

"You can't judge it by looking at it. You can only judge it by walking across it."

"Oh, come on."

"Not a good idea."

"Well, I'm going. I'm too fucking cold to walk extra hours out here." Butler gestured to David and Beryl. "And they're going to be even colder. Think they can take an extra day out here? An extra night?" He turned and walked away from them in the direction of the inlet.

The three of them watched him, the distance between them growing.

"Now this is fucked." David grimaced, watching Butler. He looked back to Jean-Claude. "Well?"

Jean-Claude stood still, regarding David. He did not answer.

"Beryl," David asked, "know anything about sea ice conditions on Hudson Bay in early winter? Want to make any suggestions?"

She and David faced each other without expression. His cheeks were flushed a mottled red.

"Well," he said, "then I say it's a risk either way. I'm cold and my thermal underwear's giving me a wedgie. Let's try the shortcut." He paced slowly after Butler.

Jean-Claude watched David walk, awkward in the snowshoes. Jean-Claude turned to Beryl, studying her as he had that first time in the airport. Beryl watched him.

He swung his snowshoes around and began to follow Butler.

CHAPTER 23

The sun rose slowly behind them, stretching their shadows out in front like elongated insects, exaggerating each awkward wobble. The snow was hard-packed at first, the sky clear, no wind. Jean-Claude said they had made good progress, four or five miles. They had no way of really knowing. The landscape didn't change, no other creatures moved upon it. They saw the tiny cloud of Churchill in the distance, but it didn't get any bigger. Their breath and the squeaking of the snow were the only sounds. The heavy sled jerked against Beryl's chest with each step, bumping across the snow behind them.

After a while, even David stopped talking about the cold. Their pace became quicker, more confident. They kept warm enough, except for their hands and faces, her feet. They stopped at noon for lunch. The meat had frozen through. They lit a fire on the large ceramic platter Jean-Claude had taken from the kitchen. They all crowded in around the warmth. Jean-Claude heaped a saucepan with snow, put it beside the fire to melt for drinking water. She couldn't feel the fire through her parka. She could sense it on her face only as dryness, as a bright light. She touched her face, no longer exactly sure what her skin was supposed to be able to feel, what gloves against her cheek had been like. Her feet had gone completely numb. She felt her weight when she stood on them as a pressure in her bones.

They held the meat over the fire on slivers of wood. None of them talked. Ten feet above them the smoke from the fire and the steam of their breath froze in the air. It hung above them, white and thick. She wondered if she stood on one of the men's shoulders and reached up, what it would feel like. A small tearing, the tinkling of broken glass.

The platter heated slowly from the fire, melted down through the drift. Snow and water slid in, putting out the flames. Butler and Jean-Claude lit the fire again, but the snow melted beneath the platter even faster. Finally they gave up trying to cook the meat slowly and simply tossed it into what remained of the fire. The beef sizzled in the boiling water and flames. The pieces were wet, charred on the outside and frozen in the center. David made a joke about Cajun-style beef. He slurred his words as though he were drunk, his lips moving too slowly. He held his chin down tight in his hood, against his chest. All of their faces were bright red except where the white spots were beginning to form. The water in the saucepan didn't get hot. It only melted, with transparent chunks of ice remaining in the center. They each drank a mugful of water from it, spitting out the ice. Beryl noticed that they all drooled a bit with their numb lips.

Everyone ate the meat as she'd been doing for several days, chewing efficiently, no conversation. She and Jean-Claude crouched together on one side of the fire, leaning against each other. A wind began to rise, sweeping in at them from the north. The sky was no longer clear. The arm that leaned against Jean-Claude was the only warm part of her. On the other side of the fire, Butler and David kept their distance from each other. Butler held the rifle across his lap, looking around carefully every few minutes. He wanted to shoot more bears. Still none came closer than half a mile, scenting the air as they passed then trotting methodically on toward the bay. While they were walking, they had all looked back now and again, searching the snow behind them.

When they packed up to leave, she kept a frozen chunk of beef in her mouth to suck on as she walked. Butler and David now pulled the sled.

That afternoon walking became much harder. The snow no longer squeaked beneath their feet, hard-packed. The edges of the snowshoes sank into the drifts if they didn't put their feet down exactly flat. They would have to struggle for balance, jerk the shoe out and walk on. The snow swirled about them at each gust of wind, stung their faces, melted in their eyes. The sled dug itself down into the powder. Every five feet Butler and David had to lift the front of the sled up and over. David couldn't lift or pull as well as Butler. At one point David slid sideways and the sled tipped. Some wood fell off. Butler cursed. David took a while getting up, wouldn't look anyone in the eye. Beryl could see a thin sheen of sweat across his face. His breath wheezed. Their hands wouldn't grasp, so it took time to pack the wood on again. Jean-Claude worked five minutes to make a knot tying the wood down. Beryl stamped around, slapped her arms against her sides. David stood still, his face sunk deep into his hood. They walked on.

She thought it was getting colder. They had no thermometer. The smudge of Churchill seemed no closer. If anything, the horizon seemed farther away. The plain of white snow stretched out in front of them, beautiful, sparkling, misleading. A mound in the foreground could turn out to be a hill many miles away or a bear sleeping much closer. Butler looked around constantly, scanned the whiteness for dots of black, the bears' noses easiest to spot from a distance. He'd swung his rifle across his back now, but he reached around often to touch its weight. Of all of them, he walked the most easily. He seemed full of energy. She could hear him sometimes sucking the air deep into his lungs as though he'd just stepped out onto his porch in the country. Jean-Claude walked on with his head down, concentrating, his feet moving smoothly.

She turned her face to the white circle of the sun, keeping her eyes open. She felt no warmth. Her eyes didn't hurt. She felt nothing.

. . .

At several points during the day, one of the men would drop back, face the way they had come and hitch down the front of his pants. Steam rose from the urine.

Early in the afternoon she couldn't wait any longer. She let them walk ahead while she crouched upon the snow, pulling down her pants. None of the men looked back. She spread her legs farther. She had to look down once to make sure she was urinating. She was no longer capable of feeling more than the general movements of her bones. Her body existed only in vision.

The warm urine melted a hole straight down through the powder. The snow had refrozen even before she stood up.

She hurried to catch up with the men.

They reached the inlet when the sun hung about halfway down the sky. Jean-Claude had them wait while he walked slowly along the edge of the broken ice, studying its color, the thickness of the shattered pieces that angled up above the others. He unpacked the sled, made three other sleds from the blankets, packing the weight of the wood and supplies evenly across all of them. He created a long leash for each blanket sled.

"It's about a mile and a half across here. I'll cross first. Butler next. David, then Beryl. Beryl," he said, "you're the lightest. You get the worst position. Take the sled. It'll spread the weight better. Ice changes thickness fast. I'm going to pick a path across the best of it. Follow me exactly. Exactly where

I walk. Drag the blankets as far behind as possible. If they start to sink, let them. Sea ice is different from freshwater ice. It gives beneath you. Don't stand still no matter what. Keep thirty feet of distance between us, the sleds far back. If one of us goes in, keep walking. Don't try to be a hero. You'll just go in too. OK?" He looked at each of them. They nodded. He looked at Beryl the longest. There was snow, she saw, in the white of his eyebrows.

Jean-Claude started out. He examined the ice, stepped slowly, smoothly onto it. Butler watched him carefully, then followed. The ice stretched out blue, gray and even yellow in places. Where the wind had pushed it together it heaved upward into walls, ramps, tabletops, small castles with spires and broken doors. The ruins of some ancient town, sparkling along the edges. Snow danced about in the wind. Butler's snowshoes skittered across the ice. He had to lean into the edges for traction. The blanket bumped along after him.

David said, "There's never a cab around when you need one." He looked slowly across the broken moon surface. "Hey, Beryl?"

She turned to him.

"Good luck, eh."

She tried to smile. She wasn't sure if her lips moved at all.

He stepped out, tracked himself carefully after Butler. When he reached the end of the leash on his blanket sled, he pulled forward into it to get the blanket sliding. She watched him, waiting, then walked after him. She couldn't tell when she'd left land and began walking on ice. The sled moved easily behind her. Its runners scratched like knives. She kept turning to look at the sled, tried to keep it on the flatter surfaces. She didn't want it spilling over on the uneven plates. Looking ahead, she could no longer see Jean-Claude. He was somewhere behind the walls of ice.

After she walked a hundred yards out, she felt the ice begin to give a little beneath her. At first it felt like she was stepping on a thick rug, then maybe Styrofoam, something stirring beneath her feet each time she shifted her weight. The feeling gradually changed to that of walking along a thick plastic plank, the material stretching out beneath her, swaying downward. She heard the cracking and popping of the crystals inside, saw a slight indent appear around her snowshoe with each step. She slid her feet forward smoothly, half-skating, her shoulders swinging with the motion. Breathing loudly with her effort, she alternately watched David's progress ahead of her and then the ice beneath her feet. She searched for the lighter streaks of ice, the gray of stone. The ice felt firmer there. Sometimes it felt completely solid. The next step could sway beneath her again. She wondered what she would do if she saw a bear out here. The bears lived on the ice most of the year. She couldn't imagine sleeping anywhere on this treacherous creaking surface.

Her sides began to itch. She rubbed her arms against her ribs. Gradually she realized she was sweating, breathing harder than she should have to for this effort. She tried to slow her breath down, to think of other things. Pushing back the hood of her parka, she could feel the wind in her sweaty hair, could see so much more clearly all around her. She felt the sweat freezing against her scalp.

She tried to get perspective on how far they were walking. A mile and a half would be the distance from her house across the river into Boston. She pretended she was stepping from her house: that ice wall was the neighbor's house, the one with the magnolia tree. That mesa top was the drugstore on the corner. She crossed the street, saw the Indian restaurant, the supermarket, the park. After a time she approached the bridge into the city. She saw the water passing below the bridge, warm and soft, the brown-blue of a temperate world. Sailboats, people tanning on the decks, their bared flesh and easy smiles. A woman in a rowboat held a beer to her cheek, the glass sweating, the liquid sloshing about inside.

Beryl imagined that by now she would have reached the other side of the river, would have reached Boston. She still couldn't see any land ahead of her. She couldn't tell if she was judging distance correctly, if she was scrolling the scenery by at the right speed. What if they were walking straight out to sea? She shuffled her feet along, scanning the ice around her.

The smoother curve of land appeared ahead. At the same instant she noticed the open break in the ice off to her left, a long gash running parallel to their path. The water steamed up into the air. They would walk within forty feet of it. The ice beneath her feet shifted colors to dark gray and then to almost black. She could see the waves shiver the ice up and down near the open water.

As she concentrated on skating in David's footsteps, something brown and heavy flitted by just beneath her feet, under the ice. She almost stumbled. The next form blinked its brown eyes as it passed beneath, its round cat face looking up at her. It flew by beneath the surface, as fast through the water as though in air, as though beneath the ice stretched a whole new world where heavy creatures could fly on their outstretched stubby hands.

"Hey," yelled David, "seals!" He stood still for a single moment, pointing down. "Check it out."

Beryl watched as the ice began to rip beneath him.

"Whoops," he said and slogged forward, but the rip followed him, rolling forward beneath his feet. She saw his motions go silky smooth, serious, as he realized the danger. The ice dipped beneath him, his snowshoes scraped for purchase. The ice tore, noisy as soggy fabric. His feet slid backward leisurely. His hands clawed out for balance.

"Butler!" screamed Beryl. "Jean-Claude, help!" She slipped out of the straps of her sled, jogged forward. With each slap of her snowshoes the surface rolled beneath her. She wasn't quite sure how she would stop when she reached him. She had no traction.

"Lie down!" Beryl yelled. "Lie across the ice."

He started to ease down, but his feet slipped. With a scratch of nylon he slid into the hole. Gone. The water glugged up against the lip.

She threw herself down, sliding across the ice toward the rip as if into home plate. She held one arm out for the far side.

The freezing water hit her flesh like a knife. Her heart

shocked still. Her arm slapped onto the other side of the ice, swung her back, the material rolling with her weight. Her head, chest and right arm lay in the water, her back and legs on the surface above. Hanging. Completely dark all around her. Her body was quiet. Death, she thought; this is what death is like.

David sank slowly just in front of her, pulled down by his billowing clothes, a fading dream. Beryl couldn't see the bottom, only blackness everywhere. A pebble clicked somewhere below her. His face gleamed very white in the gloom as he looked up at her. He blinked like a seal.

She rolled her hand through the water, grabbed the edge of his hood, surprised that her fingers could still close, could hold on. He bobbed in her grasp, reached up and took hold of her arm. He gripped hard. The ice she lay on ripped a little. The first half of her belly slid into the water. She felt the weight of her wet parka pulling her down, the weight of David. She kicked her legs out, trying to get any purchase with the edges of her snowshoes. Trying to kick the edges down into the ice, to pull up. She couldn't back out.

She and David hung together in the water looking at each other. The ice creaked again, rotten and soft in her ear.

He smiled sad and wide, let go of her slowly, shook his head. His hair rolled soft against his face. She looked at her hand wrapped hard around his hood. Her lungs began to swell against her ribs. Even if she let go, she didn't know how she would back out of the water.

The first yank on her feet shocked her so much she almost

lost her grip on his parka. Then she clenched as tight as she could and David grabbed hold of her again. He was dragged after her through the water and up, his jacket rolling around him heavy as a wet towel.

They came out gradually, pulled up onto the ice, which bent and groaned with their weight. As her head broke the water she sucked air in again and again, cranked her head around to see. Butler lay with his face buried in her ankles, his arms locked around her knees. He crawled backward, digging in with his elbows and toes. Fifteen feet beyond that Jean-Claude gripped the lashes of Butler's sled. He walked backward, straining into the weight. When they had moved twenty feet from the rip they all let go of each other, spreading out across the ice, slithering away from the danger area on their stomachs like seals, like animals groveling. After forty feet they crawled. After a hundred feet they stood up on the flat white plain of land.

CHAPTER 24

David's face was a pale blue, ice gleaming on his cheeks. His eyes blinked behind his clear mask. Beryl turned and vomited meat and dark water onto the snow by her feet. The liquid burned hot on her lips.

"Strip," Jean-Claude said to David. "Fast, everything. Butler, give him every sweater you have." Jean-Claude sat down on the snow, started to take off his outside pants. He looked at Beryl. "I told you not to be a hero. You almost killed us all. Get your jackets off. I'll give you one of mine." His face was stiff with fury.

She tried to work her arms up to pull off her jacket but couldn't seem to move her hands precisely enough to find her shoulders. David's hands slapped around loosely near his parka's zipper, making a light knocking sound against his shining chest. Butler stepped in and unzipped David's parka, stripped it off and then removed his boots. He helped David off with all his clothing, as with a baby.

Butler said, "Shit, I mean I thought the ice would be thick enough."

Jean-Claude roughly jerked both parkas over Beryl's head. She looked down at her bare breasts and stomach in the cold. Her nipples gleamed hard as plastic, ice shimmered in her belly button. Butler looked away from David's body, yanking the pants down over his heels, spilling water sluggish across the snow. David sat nude on the drift, his stomach sucked in, the hair on his head and between his legs shiny with crystals, his genitals shriveled and purple. His eyes were half-closed. His head listed. Jean-Claude took off both jackets, pulled his inner one down over Beryl's shoulders. He stood there wearing just a pair of pants. This was the first time she'd seen his chest in the daylight. He had an outie belly button. Distantly, she looked at them, all this pink tender skin against the snow. She wanted to laugh but it seemed too big an effort.

"Run." Jean-Claude said to her. "Run around us, now. Don't stop for anything."

The first few steps felt awkward, heavy. She looked down at her feet. Kicked them around in the snow to get them to behave. Her arms hung heavy as meat.

"Slap your arms. Flex your fingers. When your skin starts to hurt again wrap your hands in a blanket and keep running." Jean-Claude pulled his outer parka on. "Put David in my outer pants. Wrap blankets around his feet. I'm getting their sleds. We're going to need them." He walked smooth and fast back onto the ice, careful. He slapped his hands against his sides. The wind rolled around him and the hair of his pants shivered.

Butler rubbed at David's feet, trying to get circulation back in them. The skin looked gray and plastic. David gazed at them with his head cocked to one side and his mouth half open.

"Hey," Butler said to no one in particular, "I mean that ice should have been five feet thick by now. Don'tcha think? In this cold?" He fumbled awkwardly, pulling the pants on over David, looking away. When he had David clothed, he held him up and began to walk him around, then made him run. Without a parka, David wore several thickly knit Icelandic sweaters. Beryl thought it strange to see someone wearing a sweater out here, like it was just a fall day. Beryl could see the wind rippling the wool. The edges of David's ears were white.

When Jean-Claude came back, walking slowly across the ice, the two sleds dragging behind him, she could see the faces of three seals floating about in the open water. They watched Jean-Claude big-eyed and absorbed.

Jean-Claude picked up Beryl's Inuit parka. It had frozen with its arms held out in front, as though still reaching for David. He snapped the material twice hard against the ground. The ice tinkled off. He gave her the outside jacket, snapped clean the inside shirt to give to David to put over his sweaters.

He repacked the sled and they left with her and David

pulling it, running. Jean-Claude yelled behind them, "Faster, faster, bring your knees up."

After a while Beryl didn't want to sleep anymore. She wanted to scream from the feeling returning to her fingers and arms. She ran half-sobbing until Jean-Claude said that was enough for her and Butler took her place.

As she stepped out of the traces, she glanced at David. He stood breathing heavy with his head down, lips loose, a line of drool frozen across his chin. He hadn't spoken since they'd pulled him out of the water. Butler picked up the traces, looking at him. When Butler started jogging forward, David stumbled. Butler held his arm out to keep him standing up, moving forward.

Butler talked to him, trying to sound tough and hard as a coach. "Come on David. Keep going, you wimp. You can do it. Faster, you lazy slob." After running for a few minutes pulling the sled, he was gasping on his words.

Beryl could see he kept one hand under David's arm the whole time, keeping David moving, the sled bouncing along behind. He did not stop talking to David the whole afternoon. Once Beryl jogged in closer and she heard Butler say that David should just pretend this was all a game, imagination.

"Me and my brother," Butler gasped, trotting forward, "used to play this game all the time, pretending we were other places, other people. That's what you should do now. Like you could believe you're really in Central Park right now, walking on a hot day, near Central Park West and Seventy-sixth, sweating. Imagine you're there and just pretending to be in a cold place to forget the heat." Butler jogged on, catching his breath, then added, "Yeah, that's right. Can't you just smell the summer in the park? What is that smell anyway? Horses' turds and the grass, sweat and beer, grilling hamburgers. Can't you just smell it?" Butler watched David's face.

David never looked up from his feet slogging forward. He leaned more and more of his weight on Butler.

Beryl gasped and half-jogged behind them, her head hanging.

Near the end of that first day she tried running ahead as fast as she could. The slow jogging hurt her. She wanted to get there, to get warm, to stop moving. But her feet had no feeling and she fell and had to get up again. She pushed herself up slowly, her legs clenched, her butt waving from side to side. Her hands rolled about slack. She had to watch them to check that they moved as she wished. After that she continued to jog on at a steady pace.

That night they slept under the snow like bears. Jean-Claude scouted about for the right kind of snow. With his knife he cut the blocks out of a hard bank, built the igloo up steadily. She didn't understand how his hands could still work. His parka snapped loosely in the wind without the fur shirt beneath it. She walked about him, circling in the cold, scared to stop moving. David fell asleep quickly, dozing against a drift. The sweat had frozen shiny against his skin.

They all had breath trails iced visibly across their faces, making masks that glimmered white and hairy with frost.

Their eyes stared out like animals'. Small icicles hung from their nose hair; it tinkled and shattered under their gloves. The air she breathed had felt warm for a while now.

The trim of Butler's hood dipped down with the weight of icicles. He looked out slightly askance, from beneath, only his open mouth and chin visible. His breathing sounded slow, labored.

When Jean-Claude completed the igloo Beryl dragged David in, hooking her forearms up under his shoulders. Her hands were unable to close and grip any longer. His fur shirt hiked up. She could see the skin of his belly beneath, white-gray. He didn't wake up. She put him on the blankets in the center of the igloo, pulled the shirt down over his stomach and back, covered him with the rest of the blankets.

The blankets formed a platform in the center of the room. Jean-Claude lit a fire on the ground beside it, using the trip's journal as kindling. The wood caught quickly and the pages of the journal shriveled in the fire. Most of the pages were empty. If they didn't make it out now, Beryl thought, no one would know what had happened.

This time Jean-Claude propped the fire up on the backs of what remained of the dining room chairs. The meat thawed unevenly. It steamed, burned, blackened, filled the igloo with smoke. Her body warmed in patches, hummed, tingled. She could no longer tell where the frostbite ended and her living body began.

They ate quickly, ferociously. They couldn't wake David

up to eat. She ate until she felt her stomach push against the thongs of her pants, until her abdomen registered a dull pain.

Jean-Claude said, "We have to arrange watches for the bears." He was the only one who could speak clearly at this point. Beryl didn't understand. The bears couldn't fit in through the front entrance. The snow gleamed ice blue and warm all around them. Slowly she looked up. The roof and sides were only a foot thick.

Jean-Claude looked at her and Butler, frozen, tired, beaten. David simply huddled as a lump beneath the blankets. Jean-Claude settled for placing two rifles on top of the blankets, loaded. She knew that if the weight of the ceiling and a full-grown bear fell down on them while they slept, the guns would do them no good.

The four of them curled tightly together, between the layers of blankets icy from being dragged across the bay, the rifles hard weights above them. They had only four blankets between them and the snow they lay on. The cold rose slowly in her bones, the warmth from running gone. They kept David in the center. She and Jean-Claude hugged him tightly from both sides. Butler pushed in against her back. He breathed in her ear, put his hand on her thigh. She found it didn't bother her. She was relieved she could still feel that much. His large body warmed her back. She pushed in tighter against his heat, pulled in her arms, legs and head, breathed the air beneath the blankets. He wrapped one arm around her stomach. She curled into a small ball and slept.

During the night she woke several times. Each time she did her muscles were shivering. The fire died slowly and it got much colder. David moved around a lot at first, murmuring, talking, even screaming at one point. Later on he quieted. Then Butler became restless. Shivering, rustling, touching his face, talking to himself. She curled tighter and tighter into herself. Near morning she dreamed she was crawling once again through the storm, forward into the bend of the bear's legs. This time his fur was icy blades, the skin frozen, the bear unafraid. With a slight tinkling of ice he reached forward to scoop her tighter into his center, the cold seeping into her as clear as water.

CHAPTER 25

She overslept. The sun had risen. Jean-Claude had already left the bed, had lit the fire. He was dragging David out of the igloo by his feet. She could see only the skin of David's wrists from this angle. Thin wrists, the skin watery blue. His face turned away, his arms covering his head, his knees huddled up by his chest. The body slithered across the ice solid and still, the parka rustling.

Butler sat up beside her, his mouth slack and open, breathing in slow, his eyes surprised with new understanding.

A large mound of snow lay beside the igloo when she came out. The clothing David had worn was heaped beside it. Jean-Claude handed the sweaters back to Butler, pulled on his outer pants and fur shirt. She knew there was nothing more they could do. The ground below was frozen solid, they had nothing to dig with, but David slept under the snow already like a part of the bears.

Butler held the sweaters in his hands for a long time before putting them on. He said, "I . . . I'm sorry. God, I'm so sorry." He looked earnestly at Jean-Claude, then her. "I didn't think . . ."

Jean-Claude kept his face down, tying the waist of his pants. She noticed he looked at both of them less often now. He didn't try to stand near her or touch her, didn't offer advice. She wondered if he believed either of them would survive.

That morning they packed lighter. In the igloo they left David's gun, some of the food. Beryl looked back in. The fire still smoldered, the food lay by the gun. It seemed as though someone might return at any moment.

With two of them pulling the sled, only one of the three rested at any one time, carrying a rifle, watching for bears. Butler turned frequently to check her and Jean-Claude's faces, their energy levels. He looked around for bears less eagerly. He no longer took deep breaths, filling his lungs with the fresh air. None of them talked, not even to offer directions.

Toward midmorning the sky began to get overcast. Churchill's smudge of smoke became fuzzy, then invisible in the clouds. They came to a stop, unsure of the exact direction. This far north, any compass would only have spun lazily in its case. On this gray day, even the location of the sun was impossible to determine.

Jean-Claude stepped forward. They followed. Beryl had no

idea how he navigated. She noticed that his eyes followed the direction of the drifts about them, tracing the rise and fall of the land, moving frequently to the indistinct horizon. Sometimes he turned to look back toward where they'd come from, his face careful, concentrating, checking the direction of their path. To her eyes the land stretched tight and straight to the gray horizon, unchanging, without detail. She wondered how much the drift of snow altered the lay of the land.

To heat their lunch, they burned the tabletop. The flames warmed her face. In the heat something inside her relaxed. She could now feel the tight warmth of her chest and stomach, the harsh cold of her back. They tried the radio again and could hear static for the first time. They listened to the soft crackle as they looked off toward what Jean-Claude said was Churchill. The radio sputtered out slowly. They packed it again.

When the fire burnt down, Beryl felt much colder. Her scalp tingled. Her eyes watered. She looked down at her seated body and thought it looked like a heavy object, like carved wood. She wished she could get up without it. She looked up. The two men were standing. Jean-Claude picked up the rifle, began to scan the horizon. She noticed him sniffing the air. The sea, she thought, proud of her logic. He's trying to smell the sea. He turned his nose to the prevailing wind.

Butler stood in the traces of the sled, waiting for her. Jean-Claude turned back. She realized she hadn't yet stood up.

She moved her feet into position in front of her, pushed up. Her knees wouldn't straighten. She fell over on her face in the snow, looked up slowly to see both men watching her. Jean-Claude's face showed nothing. He looked away from her into the wind. She pushed up again. She remembered the stiffness of David's body, an object, something to be left behind. Butler and Jean-Claude could do nothing. They couldn't carry her. Her face hit the snow again. Her arms hurt from trying. She'd come so far.

Butler stepped forward, surprised her by holding out his hand. They had to try several times. Their hands had a hard time grasping. She had touched only snow for so long. His arm felt firm, different from the drifts. She tried hard. He pulled her up, overbalanced himself backward, sat down on his butt with a sigh as she stood. He pushed himself up slowly, wobbling, like a baby learning to stand. She watched him, felt fear for them both.

She walked forward into the traces of the sled with Butler. No one said a thing. They staggered a bit getting started. For the first mile he kept one hand at her elbow to make sure she did not fall. It reminded her of the way a man was supposed to lead his date into a reception, as though there was the danger of falling there too.

Later in the afternoon the toe of his snowshoe caught and he windmilled forward. She grabbed the edge of his shoulder and he stumbled against her, both their bodies striving to stay upright, awkward as logs. He caught his balance again.

The hood of his jacket nodded once, then they walked on into the weight of the sled.

She took an extra turn pulling. She warmed up. Her body felt heavy with strength, warmer than she'd ever imagined.

That evening as Jean-Claude built the igloo, she shuffled mechanically around and around the site, staring entranced at the changing colors of the clearing sky. During the day she'd gotten so used to the white of the snow, the gray of the clouds. Now with the sun setting there was orange and lilac, green and a wide belt of soft pink like the inside of a dog's ear. The shimmering drifts mirrored every color. Each small bump and depression in the snow extended long lines of shadow like thin fingers pointing the way home. She walked around and around, looking at the flat plate of the earth, the bowl of sky above. In all of it, the only break in the unearthly grace was their small awkward igloo and the trampled snow that surrounded it.

She inhaled the air, which felt warm in her lungs, held her face up to the slow blue easing its way across the heavens with the first of the stars. She did not know if any of them would make it, but she was glad, so glad she was alive.

That night the men crawled under the blankets on both sides of her. She felt their male warmth, their height and thick chests expanding against her. Her body prickled with returning feeling: prickled, hurt, screamed and raged. She heated up, grew powerful and tall.

When she woke in the morning, both men seemed smaller.

Since lunch the day before when she could not stand, she had been somewhere they had not. She looked at the exit to the igloo, to the snow and cold sunshine. She wanted to get outside, to stand again under that clear blue sky.

Butler crawled out of the igloo first. Jean-Claude followed, then Beryl. She kept looking up at the sky. Butler stood back from them and the igloo, watching with the gun while they crouched over the blankets, strapping everything back together. He stood tall, big, the gun jutting out from his hip. He scanned this world from the stance of a hunter.

The bear stepped out from behind the igloo, ten feet from Beryl and Jean-Claude, Butler on the far side. It moved slowly, curious, scenting the air. It looked at them, the bones of its shoulders tall and thin, its skin raw at the elbows. Against that huge white world it looked like a starving alley cat.

She and Jean-Claude froze, down low over the sled, watching. Butler stepped forward, waving the rifle. Beryl saw that he felt pity for the thin bear, meaning to frighten it. "Hey," he barked. "Shoo. Go away."

The bear lunged. Beryl wasn't sure what happened. The world was white. The body was white. It flew by Jean-Claude, flew around her. She felt one of its claws pinch all its weight into her foot. The gun discharged once, wildly. The bear hit Butler.

"Shit." She heard Butler's voice quite clearly.

The sound of a wet wooden crack. He fell. His neck tilted.

The bear reached its mouth down slowly and bit into his cheek, pulled back and started to chew. Butler's throat rattled. The bear put its paw on his chest. The air heaved out wet from his lungs, then silence. His limbs loosened. The animal reached forward again.

Jean-Claude and Beryl stepped slowly backward, holding the rope of the sled. The sled swayed across the snow, rustled, clanked. The bear looked up at them, her face splattered in blood. Her ear twitched. The silence hung vibrant. Jean-Claude and Beryl backed away from the bear. She let them go.

Beryl saw more bears approaching from nowhere, spots of white and yellow trotting forward from all directions toward the new meat.

She thought she should cry but mostly she felt surprise, disbelief. Each blink of her eyes took effort, seemed to make a click somewhere near her ears.

Beryl and Jean-Claude left more things behind at their lunch site. Some meat, three blankets, the sled, a gun. They tied the remaining things into a single blanket and dragged it along behind. Jean-Claude moved very slowly, his limp more pronounced. He kept his left hand clasped in his armpit, then took it out, shook it, blew into the wrist of the mitten, punched his hand into his leg. The afternoon turned cloudy again. When she looked back, she could see the lunch camp for a long time. Jean-Claude wouldn't look at her at all. They didn't talk. She felt completely alone. She no longer tried to brush her shoulder against his as they walked. It seemed too much of an effort.

They had only one gun left. It slapped against Jean-Claude's back as he pulled the blanket sled, interfering, slowing him down. Finally, he tied it into the blankets and walked on. She listened to her own breath, the creak of the snow beneath her feet. She stared down at the brown of her caribou pants, the left leg then the right swinging into view as she marched, the light wood of the snowshoes, the gray trim on her boots and the bright yellow on their sides spelling out NATURAL PHOTOGRAPHY. The bold letters in bumblebee gold seemed from another universe. Such a vivid color, such small distinct forms.

She remembered when she had said good-bye to her parents, clasping her mother against her, the feel of the bra straps obvious through the thin shirt, the soft flesh and the bones inside. Her father standing back awkward, covering his face with the camera until it was his turn. She looked up and around for more bears.

It began to snow. She walked on through it, keeping pace with Jean-Claude's stride, listening to the rustle of the fur against her skin and the creak of her shoes until she could not hear as well through the rising wind. The snow came down faster. She realized she was losing sight of her feet through the shifting snow. Jean-Claude stopped and she stumbled to a halt beside him. He turned around in the storm, scuffed his foot into the snow beneath them, examining the texture. She couldn't see more than a white round room about them, the same in every direction. Jean-Claude pulled off suddenly to the left. They walked single file. The wind rose. The room shrank. Her eyes squinted, snow built up on her face. She followed him. For a sense of time, of distance, she counted her own breaths. She got to five hundred. She was pretty sure by that time that she had begun to count slower, to breathe slower, that time was changing.

She could no longer see the end of the sled rope she followed.

The rope stopped, dipped down. Jean-Claude was hunkered down, an outline as soft as gray mist in the snow, digging. She reached out cautiously and touched the fur of his hood, pushed it a little to the side to see his face. She'd thought she would be alone with the rope until her will gave out. He looked at her, startled. Human eyes looked strange after so much snow. She touched her glove to his cheek. He watched her blankly, then something softened. He brushed the back of his glove against her lips.

Turning away, he tunneled straight into the snow, hollowing out a ditch on the far side of the wind. They sat in the hole, held a blanket up as a roof to keep back the snow, leaning against each other. The blanket grew heavy above her head, darkening as snow piled above. The air stilled within their hole, closed off. The sound of the wind dulled. She warmed up. She could see nothing. She felt his leg across her foot. She was trying to remember the exact sound of summer rain on leaves, in puddles on the earth. They held the roof up until at some point her head nodded forward. When she woke her arms were still pushing up.

Later she woke again. She lay curled round Jean-Claude,

warm. She sat up, her body moving easily in their quiet den. She rummaged around in the dark, found the meat. The air was thick with the smell of human sweat and meat, stuffy. She ate. Chunks fell from her mouth. She touched the skin of her arms, legs, neck. She was warm, she could feel. Her fingers ran across the walls. They steamed wet with the heat, the ceiling the rough texture of the blanket. She searched Jean-Claude's body, found his face. With each breath something clicked within his throat. She leaned down very carefully, matching the outline of his mouth with hers. She kissed him. Again. He laughed beneath her, that soundless pant. Their lips lay slack against each other; she could feel the kiss only in the roots of her teeth. They pushed together, miming passion. Pressed tight and awkward, turning their heads from side to side, letting go. They pulled their bodies slowly into each other's curves, so close they could feel each other's bellies filling with breath. She felt warm. They slept.

She dreamed she was pregnant. She looked into the face of her child and saw a strong happy woman looking back into her mother's old lair with pride.

She struggled awake. The walls were iced solid, pitch black, no air. Her head felt fuzzy, slow. She heard Jean-Claude's hoarse breath, felt her own within her chest. She woke him, had to shake him hard. He had trouble sitting up. She fumbled for the knife on his belt, held it tight, swung to the side of the den where there was no blanket, chipping at the ice. Cold chunks hit her face. Tiny lights swayed in front of her. She threw her arm fast into each chip. She couldn't tell if the lights were real. Her arm didn't want to move. It wanted to sleep again. She clenched the knife with her other arm, drove outward. The wall sighed, air whispered down onto them. She breathed deeply, widened the hole.

Jean-Claude managed to sit up. The lights disappeared. She breathed deeply. Now she drove upward with the knife, at an angle, packing the snow down beneath her and crawling over it. A handful of snow fell with a sigh onto her face. She wiped it off. She'd forgotten how cold it could be. Her face tingled. Jean-Claude pulled himself up behind her, bumping against her feet. She dug farther out of the den, pulled herself up. She began to use her hands against the snow. No light showed through. For a while she wondered if she was really heading upward. She imagined them on the side of a mountain, tunneling along the angle of the slope. Their breaths wheezed, the only noise, the snow smooth beneath their hands.

As soon as she could see light, snow slapped down again across her face. This snow had weight; it pushed onto her face like a hand, held her down like a body. Snow blocked her nose and mouth, held her arms back against her sides. She tried to force them straight up. They didn't move. She remembered her dream of the child. She snaked her fingers, her hands, her arms slowly through the snow, forward, inch after inch. Patient, calm. Held her breath. Snow melted down into her mouth, tickled her nostrils, cold water. Jean-Claude tapped against her feet, not knowing what had happened. If she suffocated, she knew he would climb out over her body. She wanted to breathe the water. She wanted to suck in the snow. The lights reappeared. Her hand touched her own face. She cupped the snow away. Air. Breathed raggedly, then deep and strong. She pushed up one more time. Beryl broke from the snow into the morning like the bears she had seen. The sun. The sky was clear, the air as clean and blue as that first morning in Churchill.

Jean-Claude crawled out beside her. They had slept ten feet down, on the side of a drift a hundred feet wide. He had brought only the rifle with him, dragging it along by its strap.

Neither wanted to go back down into the den even for the meat. They could see the town in the distance—roofs, walls, spots of color. Tiny cars puttering slowly about.

"Not more than four miles," Jean-Claude said. His voice sounded hoarse, unused. She still had not spoken. He looked at her more easily now, no longer doubting she would live. She felt strong.

They shuffled quickly through the snow. Their throats rasped. She felt her leg muscles clenching and pushing. She saw herself plowing through the snow with the grace of a caribou, the power of a polar bear. Her blood coursed certain and hot. She looked over at one point and realized that Jean-Claude couldn't keep up. His limp had become more pronounced; he was slowing down.

She heard the sigh of snow beneath him as he fell. It took her several steps to stop, to turn back. He lay on his back where he had fallen, just lying and breathing. He gazed at his right foot, perplexed.

"Damn," he said and tried getting up. He moved each limb in turn, with concentration, then gradually pulled himself up to a sitting position. She reached down, grasped his arms and tried to pull him up. Looking at his right boot she wondered if his foot was hanging strangely. She could not really tell through the thickness of its material. Her left knee crumpled beneath her. She took a step forward and recovered her balance. She thought if she fell she would not be able to get back up either.

He let go of her, pulled the gun off his back, set it across his lap and scanned the area around them.

"Get help," he said, his words slurred as if he were drunk. She nodded, watched him for a moment and then turned away. It took her several minutes to get the rhythm back in her stride. She was half-running again. Looking over her shoulder, she could see him receding in the distance. He sat on the ground, flapping his arms up and down, half of a jumping jack, trying to keep warm. She quickened her pace. Ahead, she saw a truck drive out of town toward the airport. In the quiet she could hear its gears grind as it shifted. Farther away a door slammed, a child laughed. She tucked her head into her hood, tried to go faster.

She arrived in town, the sun bright above. She marveled at the vividness of the houses, the colors of the doors and curtains and cars. Reds, purples, blues, greens. Sharp solid angles, textures. So much vibrant life in such a compressed space, such a tiny curtailed place. Walls, roads, corners. A bear passed her on the street, looked her over, walked on. She held no rifle, felt no fear.

She walked toward a bright growing green, the painted door of a house. She'd never seen such a beautiful color as this green, never seen such brilliance. She pulled herself up the seven stairs to the door, one step at a time. Her knees wouldn't bend, her hands wouldn't grasp. She hooked her forearms through each railing and levered herself up. The door stood in front of her. She'd never seen anything so neat and cleanly defined, the door frame painted bright blue. She fumbled with her gloves, trying to pull them off, then gave up and pushed the buzzer with her elbow. A chime, electronic, sounded high and clear. She heard voices inside.

Even at noon, a light clicked on above her. She blinked into the tiny glitter of its coil. She looked down again at the door, at its emerald green, its smooth wood knob and small iron basket with yellow plastic flowers.

The door began to open. She thought to herself, How small it all is.